IN THIS MOMENT

A SWEETS HIGH ROMANCE

AMY SPARLING

First Edition September 2017

Cover design by Amy Sparling

CHAPTER ONE

Clarissa

"YOU DON'T HAVE to hold onto me," Grandpa says, pushing my arm away. "I've walked this path a million times this summer," he goes on, grumbling to himself as he takes an uneasy step forward.

I stay close to him, watching his feet amble over the grass, ready to catch him should he fall.

And then he stumbles. I grab his arm. "Grandpa! Go slower!"

He curses under his breath, then looks up at the bright autumn sky. He stops walking, and just stands here for a second. I'm still holding onto his arm, but he doesn't shove me off.

"Clarissa," he says after a moment. I think he's going to mention the greenhouse, but he goes the opposite way. "You get yourself to the eye doctor once a year, you hear me?"

"Yes, sir," I say. "I know."

"Every year. Don't skip it because you feel fine. You make sure you go."

"I will."

Grandpa is only sixty-five, but he has glaucoma. Apparently, he knew he had the beginning stages of it years ago, but he never went to the doctor until it got too bad. Glaucoma is an eye disease that slowly makes you go blind, but if the doctors catch it early enough, they can give you treatments to prolong your vision for several more years. Grandpa got the treatments too late.

He was still able to get around most of this summer, but his eyesight has been declining more and more. It's worse in the sunlight, so even though we're just walking from the daycare parking lot to the greenhouse at the back of the playground, he needs me to help stop him from falling.

"What's she look like?" Grandpa says after I've maneuvered him a few steps closer to our masterpiece. *She* is what he calls the greenhouse.

"She's glorious," I say, tipping my head up to look at the beautiful ten foot by ten foot structure. "We did a great job."

"*You* did a great job." He pats me on the back. "Those kids are gonna be so happy."

I grin. This whole summer project started because I got my heart broken, although I'd like to say it's become more than that over the last few weeks.

After my jackass ex-boyfriend Shawn decided he didn't like dating a girl who was as tall as me—literally, that's what he said—I was understandably crushed. I wish he would have lied and said he didn't like my personality or something. But no, he told the truth, which hurt more than anything.

Shawn was my first real boyfriend. As in, he *asked* me to be his girlfriend, and we went on dates and made out and I let him grab my boobs even though he wasn't very good at it. I liked him though. I liked him a lot. We were exactly the same height, and he hated it. At five foot ten inches, I'm always the tallest girl anywhere I go. It's something that's always bothered me, but when Shawn asked me to be his girlfriend I thought it would all be okay.

Of course, I was stupid to think that.

After crying for twenty-four hours straight, I'd gone searching for something to take my mind off being heartbroken. I landed on a box of old black and white photographs from my grandparent's younger years. My grandma was a beautiful woman with a heart shaped face and a smile that made you want to smile back. I only know these things from photographs. She died when I was three, so I have no memories of her at all.

Shortly after, Grandpa moved in with me and Mom so he wouldn't have to live alone. Since my own dad died when I was also a baby, Grandpa is the closest thing to a father that I've ever had.

I was going through the old photos when I saw a stack of them that pictured Grandma showing kids around a greenhouse. It's was small and rickety even back then, but the kids looked unbelievably happy to be in there among the fresh flowers and exotic plants.

I'd asked Grandpa about the photos and he told me that greenhouse was Grandma's favorite thing. She spent her entire life working at the daycare that she owned next to the high school. After she'd retired, she'd sold the place to someone else, but it's still a daycare.

I realized that greenhouse was still there at the back of the playground, covered in overgrown weeds and slowly rotting to the ground. I decided I wanted to rebuild it in my grandma's memory.

Anything to get my mind off this heartache.

Mrs. Bradley is the new owner, and since I work there during the summers, she was happy to let me build the greenhouse back again. She said the kids would love it, and she even gave me the money to buy the materials.

Grandpa did all the hard work, like building the frame and cutting the material with his huge bandsaw, but I put it all together with him, doing more and more of the work as his eyesight slowly faded away. This is our masterpiece, and now it's finally done.

Grandpa puts a hand on the green paneled wall. "She's a beaut," he says, but his eyes are squinted so much I know he probably can't see it at all.

"Thanks for all your help," I say as I admire the little house. It's now ready for pots and bags of mulch, and soon we can plant flowers and it'll be inspiring these kids just like it did when my grandma worked here.

Grandpa throws an arm over my shoulder. "I'll let you guide me back to the car," he says, sounding somewhat resigned. "I'm so proud of you, Clarissa. Your grandmother would be too."

Despite my best efforts in choosing a soft, mellow tune on my phone, when the alarm goes off at six-thirty in the freaking morning, that sound is what nightmares are made of. I groan and roll out of bed, wondering how the hell I've survived so many years of school before now.

Only two more left, and today is the first day of my junior year of high school.

Blah!

I spent most of my summer being heartbroken, and yet it still went by too fast. Rolling my eyes, I throw on some jeans, a new pair of running shoes, and a purple tank top. Then I grab a sweater because even though it's a million degrees outside in this Texas heat, usually the classrooms are freezing.

Mom smiles at me from the kitchen, where she's eating a bowl of cereal. She's not tall. She's just average height. I got all my tall genes from my dad. "Hi, baby," she says. "Haven't seen you this early in *months*."

She laughs at her joke. I don't know what I'll do when I graduate and have to get a real job working all year long. Summer breaks are amazing and everyone should get them.

I grab some toast and head out the door in just enough time to catch the bus. The stupid thing is five minutes earlier than it was last year. On the ride to school, I study my new schedule. They changed things up this year. Now we all have a fifteen minute homeroom class at the start of the day before our real classes begin. It sounds stupid, but oh well. The homeroom class is supposed to be where they make the morning announcements and the teacher will pass out any important papers. We are all put in classes based on last names, so as a Vale, I'm at the end of the alphabet.

My best friend Livi Garner will be in another homeroom, and to our epic dismay when we discussed schedules the other day, we have no freaking classes together. Not even lunch. She's first lunch and I'm second lunch, so at most, we'll see each other before and after school for just a few minutes.

This year is already total crap.

Livi waits for me in the bus drop off lot. Her long golden

hair has been curled in big waves that fall around her shoulders. Her makeup is also on point, and I wonder how the girl wakes up so early to get all dolled up each day. Unlike some people, she doesn't just do this for the first day of school. She does it every day. It's sort of inspiring.

"Hey," she says, joining me in the walk to hell's gates, er, I mean school.

"Blahhhh," I say back. She laughs.

"Your greenhouse looks awesome."

I glance to the right, where you can barely see the daycare which is next to the high school. A little green square hovers in the distance in the land between the two buildings.

"I'm pretty excited for it," I say.

"Okay don't freak out, but look at me," Livi says, her voice suddenly alarmed.

Of course that makes me look over. "Don't!" she repeats, grabbing my arm. "Look at me! And laugh like I'm telling a hilarious joke."

I try to smile, but it's too late. I've accidently seen Shawn in the crowd of students. He's looking gorgeous as always, his amber hair gelled back, his bright green eyes smiling right at—ugh—Mindy.

I can't help but watch as she slides her stupid arm around his back and he does the same, loping a long arm over her petite shoulders.

Mindy is very tan, and very cute, with long brown hair that has blue tips. She's like a hot gothic girl, and if I'm recalling correctly, she's also totally rich. I've never hung out in her friend group, but she has parties with her other rich friends a lot.

None of that bothers me, though. The very clear and

present fact is that my ex left me for a girl who is very short. I bet he loves the way he can throw his arm around her shoulders and look down at her like she's some stupid, tiny princess. He hated when I wore anything other than flipflops or flats because he didn't want me looking taller than he was.

It's not like I can help how tall my freaking bones want to grow.

"Rissa, stop it," Livi hisses in my ear. Her fingers dig into my arm and she steers me down a side hallway, doing her best friend duty to pull me away from staring at my idiotic ex.

I sigh and lean back against the cool painted brick wall. "Thanks."

"I got you," she says. Livi is also short. It never bothered me until now. Now I hate every short girl ever. Okay, maybe not my best friend, but the rest of them.

"You, stay strong," she says, unaware of my evil thoughts against short girls. "This is a new school year and we're going to rock it. Don't worry about that asshole and his stupid new girlfriend."

I force a smile. "You're right. I won't."

We break off when the bell rings and head to our homeroom classes. Mine is in a room in the art hallway, and the teacher, Mrs. Lin, is this older woman with extra thick glasses. She teaches a class on art history, so it's like the most boring art class there is. You don't make anything in here, you just learn. Luckily, I'm only here for homeroom.

Mrs. Lin stands at the door, smiling as we enter. "Your name is on your assigned seat," she says to everyone who walks in. I head to the row with the few other V last names and find Vale written on a post-it note on the desk that's supposed to be mine.

Only the asshole with Voss written on his post-it note is already sitting in the chair behind me, his big stupid feet laid out on my chair as if it's his own personal ottoman.

He doesn't even notice me stop in front of my desk and stare at him. He's a jock, a soccer player by the looks of his stupid black hoodie with the soccer team logo on it. He's chatting with two other equally stupid soccer players who are sitting in the next row.

I clear my throat.

He doesn't even look over.

"Excuse you," I say, loud enough to get his attention. "Your feet are on my chair."

His eyes meet mine. They're a bright blue, and would match his short brown hair nicely if he wasn't a stupid jock douche. Shawn is a jock, a baseball player to be exact, and because of him I now hate not only every short girl, but every jock as well.

"What's the magic word?" he says. He gives me this stupid smirk like he's stupid enough to think I'm going to ask him nicely to move his feet off my chair. And to make matters worse, his stupid friends laugh like this is all some funny game. I'm tired of playing games with guys.

I sling my backpack off my shoulders, and swoop it down, using it to knock his feet off my chair in one quick motion. "The magic word is get the hell off my desk," I say.

And then I sit down, ignoring the laughter from his idiot friends.

CHAPTER TWO

GAVIN

DAMN.

I watch the girl drop into her seat, her brown hair swishing in place behind her. Shoulders back, she stares straight ahead like she doesn't give one single shit about what she just did. That's kind of hot.

For some reason, my mind flashes to my mom, and something she said not too long ago.

"One of these days, some girl is going to give you back some of the shit you dish out," she'd said.

It was after some blonde chick on the softball team had approached my mom at her late night shift at the local Wal-Mart and told her I was mean. Mom always thinks it's cool when my school friends talk to her at work, but this time she was annoyed.

Maybe she was right though. Maybe some girls won't put up with my shit.

I admire the back of her head for a few seconds, and then lean forward, trying to think of something to say. I'm about to tap her shoulder when the teacher slams the classroom door closed and walks to the front of the class.

"The bell has rung," she says. "That means all talking will cease and all eyes will look forward."

Geez. I'm glad I only have this class for fifteen minutes every day.

The teacher, whatever her name is, explains about homeroom this year. She says we will report to her class promptly and we won't speak because fifteen minutes isn't very long and we need to get all of the valuable information the school wants to tell us each day.

I chuckle under my breath because the only thing valuable the school could tell me is when the holidays are. A dark feeling falls over me as I realize that days off from school used to be the greatest thing ever. Now, I actually don't mind being here eight hours a day, and longer on game days. Home has become a place I'd rather not be, at least without Mom there. Dad's drinking problem has gone from annoying to downright pissing me off lately. And there's nothing I can do. Mom tells me to let it go. She says just let him do his thing and stay out of his way. So long as Dad is still going to work every day, still bringing home the paychecks we need to survive, then we're fine.

I say screw that. Mom shouldn't have to put up with his drunken bullshit every night before she goes to work. She works the night shift, and she sleeps during the day. But now she barely sleeps at all if Dad is home, because all he does is drink, yell, and be a bastard.

She says he's harmless because he's just an angry drunk, not a violent one. But we both know there's a line there, and should my dad ever cross it, I will too.

The girl in front of me stares straight ahead, taking notes in a pink spiral. She doesn't look over at anyone and she doesn't talk. She must be one of those types that follows the rules.

I lean back in my chair while the teacher goes on and on about school expectations and all that other shit. I stare at the girl in front of me. Why haven't I seen her before? Sweets High isn't that big of a place. Maybe she's new.

Maybe I should offer to walk her to her next class. I glance over and see my teammates Beau and TJ, both looking bored as hell. If they see me try to talk up this girl, they'll give me hell for it.

I decide to keep my mouth shut.

After soccer practice, TJ and Beau ask if I wanna hit up the Lone Star Diner for some burgers. As much as I'd love one of those damn burgers, with extra cheese and curly fries, I say no.

I have car insurance, a cell phone bill, and gas to put in my truck, all of which I have to pay for myself. I worked my ass off all summer, mowing lawns and delivering pizzas, and that money has to last. Unlike my dickhead friends, my parents don't have any cash to spare for me. We all pay for ourselves at my house, and since soccer takes up most of my time once school starts, I'll be lucky if I work two or three nights a week at Magic Mark's Pizza.

"Why the hell not?" TJ asks, slamming his fist on the hood of my truck. "Burgers!"

"Burgers!" Beau says, louder. Some other guys from the

team walk by and shout burgers too. Now it's an all-out burger yelling match.

I shrug it off. "I got shit to do at home, man. I'll see you tomorrow."

"He ain't got shit to do," Beau says.

"What, you got some homework?" TJ adds, rolling his eyes. "You suddenly a teacher's pet?"

I laugh. There's no way I'm telling them I need to save my money for more important things. So I lie. "If by homework, you mean a girl, then yeah."

"Damn, bro." TJ taps my hood again, this time giving me a look of appreciation. "Get the hell out of here then."

I wish I was going home to meet a girl.

When I get home, I pull my truck next to Dad's and cut the engine, sitting here for a minute. The lights are on in the living room, and the sound of my dad's favorite Metallica album is flowing out of the house. At least it's not cranked up as loud as it goes, which gets the cops called on us.

Dad must be okay, I decide.

When I go inside, he's sitting on the couch, a beer in one hand and a plate of nachos in the other. "Hey," he says, nodding at me as I walk by.

"Hey," I say back. Nice and calm, and he won't get upset.

Sometimes I wish we'd get him some help. Send him to a rehab center or something. But unlike most of the privileged assholes I go to school with, my parents aren't loaded. We have a decent three-bedroom brick home that looks nice on the outside. It's a remnant of the days when both of my parents were happier and Dad worked in the oilfield making a ton of money. But as his alcoholism got worse, he got laid off more and more, and ended up getting a job with a small roofing company that doesn't pay much at all. Mom had to start working again when I was about twelve, and she chose to work nights because it pays more.

I got a job the day I was legally allowed to work, and together we stay afloat as a family. I just wish there was more money to get Dad some help, not that I'll ever say it. He'd really lose his shit then.

I shower and make a sandwich. Dad's phone rings, and from the other room, I can hear him talking to what sounds like my Uncle Chase.

Shit.

Sure enough, Dad's voice goes from a little annoyed to full out angry. Uncle Chase is the only family member who isn't afraid to call Dad on his shit. I hear Dad cursing on the phone, calling his brother every name in the book.

Slowly, I grab another soda from the fridge, and slip off to my room undetected. But the yelling only gets worse. When Dad hangs up the phone with a few choice expletives, I hear him pacing around the living room, still muttering about his brother, not that anyone is there to listen.

"Thinks he's better than me," Dad mutters.

I stand by my bedroom door, wondering if I should do something but from past experience, I know it's better to just keep my mouth shut.

The fridge opens and I hear the clank of another beer bottle opening. Another metal cap clinking to the counter top.

Dad cranks the music louder.

Eventually, the music is so loud it's shaking the walls, and I know the cops will probably roll up at any moment, and my dad will curse at them too. They're all pretty good with people like my dad, taking his insults in stride, but I'm not the only one worried that one day his stupidity will land him in jail.

If he's not working, then we're not getting all the bills paid. Mom and I would be screwed.

Sure enough, red and blue lights flash through my window a few minutes later. Shit. I throw on a shirt and some flipflops and run out the front door past my dad who is drinking on the couch, swaying to the music.

"Officers, I'm so sorry," I say as soon as they get out of their cars. "I'll make him turn down the radio."

One of the officers, a short woman with her hair pulled back in a tight bun, gives me a sad smile. She's been here before, and she probably remembers it. "Why don't we go inside and help you?"

I know there's no point in arguing.

As soon as Dad sees the cops enter our house, he stands up and throws his beer to the floor where it spills out all over the rug.

"Narc!" he yells at me. "Worthless!"

"I didn't call the cops on you, Dad. The neighbors did."

He glares at me like he doesn't believe it. An officer reaches behind the stereo and pulls the plug, then holds it up so my dad can see it. "No music after seven p.m. You understand?"

"That ain't no law," Dad spews.

"It is for you," the female officer says. "Noise complaints are made about this house several times a week. I don't want to take you to jail. I don't even want to write you a ticket. Just keep the music off."

They leave, and Dad doesn't put up a fight.

He just waits until the two cop cars drive away and then he glares at me. "You're a useless piece of shit," he says, his words slurring together so badly that if I hadn't heard him say that so many times before, I might not have understood it.

"I know," I say, not in the mood to argue with him. "You should take a hot shower. Maybe go to bed."

"Don't tell me what to do." He picks up the beer bottle from the rug and flings it at me. Luckily his aim is so bad it just crashes against the wall, leaving drops of beer on the paint.

"You're the worst son on the planet."

I head back to my room. I sit on my bed. I stare at the wall. I tell myself to let his drunken words bounce right off me, but they never do. I flash back to playing soccer with him in the back yard when I was five. Christmases and family vacations back when we were happy and Dad wasn't a drunk. Maybe if he'd been this shitty my whole life, it wouldn't matter. But he hasn't. I still have the good memories, and they're what makes the new memories even worse.

It's already after ten o'clock, but I don't care. I call up TJ, and they're still at the diner. "I'll be there in five minutes," I say.

Louetta, Texas is a small town with only one main street. That's where the high school is, along with other businesses, shopping centers, and the Lone Star Diner. I sit in the booth with my friends, telling them I'm not hungry, and stare out the window at the high school across the street.

Beau has been sneaking sips from a flask all night and he's more than drunk by the time I arrive.

At midnight, they kick us out because the diner is closing, and we all decide that Beau can't drive his sorry ass home since he's too drunk. I offer to drive him, just so I don't have to go home so soon.

"Dude," Beau says as he stumbles through the parking lot. "We should like, set the school on fire." He wiggles his eyebrows as he gazes at the school across the street. "That way we don't have to go back."

"That's arson," I say, opening the truck door for him. He better not throw up in my truck. "You'd go to jail for that."

Beau stumbles forward, looks at my truck and then turns around. "But I wanna destroy something," he says.

I am not in the mood to shove his ass into my truck, but it's looking like I will have to. "Get in," I say.

He shakes his head. And then he takes off running.

The idiot can sure run like hell even when he's drunk. That's the true skill of a soccer player, I guess. I chase after him, across the highway that's empty of cars because it's so late, and into the high school parking lot.

"You're not setting the school on fire," I say. "You don't even have a lighter."

"I want to destroy something," he says, holding his fists in the air. "I am a man and I want to be manly."

I snort out a laugh. He's a complete idiot when he's drunk. Beau's gaze focuses on a greenhouse in the distance. "Bingo," he says. He takes off running again.

I follow him to the little greenhouse at the edge of the school's property. There's a daycare next door, so it's closed. The school is closed too, but I get this weird feeling like we might be watched.

"Let's go," I say, halfway debating if I should just leave him here.

He picks up a hammer on the ground. "Perfect."

He swings it at the greenhouse and the plastic green wall cracks open. Beau's satisfied laugh fills the air.

"Dude."

I stand here, half annoyed and half envying him. He swings again, and again, breaking out pieces of the walls. His laughter gets louder. "It's not arson, bro!" he says as he swings again and a large piece of the wall breaks off.

He hands me the hammer. "Your turn!"

I look around. This hunk of junk has been here forever. There's an old pile of green plastic panels stacked up to the side, and tools are in a bucket next to the door. I look inside. The place is empty. Clearly no one cares about this place. They're probably going to tear it down anyhow.

I think about my dad and let the anger fill me up. Then I swing at the wall and the hammer takes out a chunk of it. Beau whoops and I feel laughter rising in my own chest.

I'm not drunk like he is, but this is euphoric.

I take a deep breath and swing the hammer again.

CHAPTER THREE

Clarissa

I FOLD my binder closed and let out a sigh. The first day of school is supposed to be easy. For most of my life, it's been easy. But not junior year, apparently. All of my teachers passed out this stupid "About Me" worksheet that they want us to fill out and return tomorrow.

There's seven classes a day, and like twenty five students per class. I really doubt these teachers are reading every single worksheet about all their students. There's just no way. And even if they did, it's not like they'd remember everything. They give us this crap to torture us.

But now I'm finally done writing about my favorite food and color and other pointless things that will never matter in the classroom. Livi has been texting me nonstop ever since she got named on Instagram as one of the girls with the best hair. It's so unbelievably stupid, but a couple years ago, these girls started rating people online, trying to make it into a thing. I guess now it *is* a thing. I've never been chosen for anything, which is fine by me. I'd rather not have the attention of everyone, online or in person.

I grab my phone and reply to Livi's text about if she should spend the money to get a blowout at the salon this weekend.

I tell her no, because her hair looks gorgeous naturally.

She writes back: *um, excuse you. This isn't natural...I work really hard on it!*

I send her the eye rolling emoji.

"Clarissa!" my mom's voice rings out.

I poke my head outside of my bedroom door. "What's up?"

"Can you give me a hand?" She holds out two large bags from Home Depot. Inside are two dozen lights that plug into wall outlets. They're motion sensors, according to the packaging.

"What is this?" I ask.

"Motion lights," she whispers back. Whispering is what she does when she doesn't want Grandpa to overhear. Now, it makes sense. He's finding it harder and harder to move around the house now, even though he has the layout memorized.

"I'll take this side of the house," I say, ripping open the packages.

Together, we go through, placing a motion light in the outlets all around the house. Grandpa is sleeping on the recliner in the living room, so I tip toe around him and plug in some more lights.

By the time we're done, we turn off all the lights in the house and then test it out. Like magic, as you walk down the hall, the lights turn on and light your path.

"This is pretty cool," I say.

"I don't know how long it'll help," Mom says, a frown wrinkling her lips. "But it's something."

We've barely talked about what we'll do when Grandpa loses all of his sight. We don't want him to go in a nursing home, mostly because it's sad, and also because we know he would hate that. But it's also scary thinking of leaving him here by himself while we're at work and school. Sometimes at night, I'll close my eyes and try to walk the house by memory. I'm much younger and more agile than Grandpa, and yet I still crash into things when I can't see.

Mom thinks he'll be fine if he uses a cane and just stays in the living room while we're not home.

I worry that won't be enough. I'd hate to come home one day and discover that he'd fallen and hurt himself.

After testing out the lights, I find Grandpa in the living room and I get him to hold my hand while I walk him around the house. He says he can see the lights, and they kind of help.

"Clarissa," he says after our third trip around the house. "I think I'm ready for bed. Can you take me to my toothbrush?"

I walk him into his room, which is the master bedroom. Mom gave it to him when he started losing his sight, saying it'd be better for him to have a big room with its own bathroom.

Before I leave, Grandpa squeezes my hand. "Clarissa, I am so proud of you," he says. I don't know how much he can actually see of me, but his eyes look into mine with a grandfatherly sort of admiration. "Those kids are going to love that greenhouse."

"Well, it's not ready yet," I say as dread weighs me down,

making me sigh. "We still have to actually plant the flowers, and I have no idea how to keep something alive."

Mrs. Bradley was excited about the greenhouse when I pitched the idea to her, but she also said I'd get to be in charge of the whole thing. She said she doesn't have a green thumb, and well, I have no idea if I have one. I've never tried to grow anything. The first time I was given a bouquet of flowers, it died after a couple of days because I didn't realize it came with flower food you had to mix into the water.

"You'll do fine," Grandpa says. "Get a pack of seeds, plant them, and water once a day. That greenhouse will be flourishing before you know it."

I grin, and then put his hand on the bathroom door frame so he can feel his way around. "Goodnight, Grandpa."

I know I won't be able to fall asleep easily tonight, so I just lay in bed and stare at the blank TV screen in the corner of my room. I spend half an hour flipping through Netflix but nothing sounds good to watch. I can't really describe the feeling in my chest. It's something like a cross between dread and anxiety, and I don't even know why.

My greenhouse is done. All we have left to do is haul away the old pieces and pack up the tools, and Mom said she'd help me with that this weekend since Grandpa is now too blind to be helping me haul stuff.

But as I lay here, feeling weirdly anxious and full of dread, I wonder if building the greenhouse was the easy part. I had been so excited to recreate my late grandmother's dream, that I hadn't stopped to realize what comes after that step.

Planting freaking flowers.

I've even measured out the shelves and decided how

many clay pots we need to buy, but I haven't put much thought into what plants we'll use yet. I figured that once school started, and I drop my daycare work hours down to two days a week, I can ask the kids what they'd want. We'll take a vote, and let them choose what to plant. Now, I'm thinking that's not a good idea. I'd hate to get their hopes up and then plant something I can't grow. Instead, maybe I'll research what the easiest, foolproof plants are, and use those.

All of these stupid greenhouse worries are just covering what's really keeping me awake.

I roll over in my bed and pull the comforter up to my face, wishing I could block out my thoughts as easily as I can close out my bedroom around me by putting a blanket over my head. It only took one day of school to run into Shawn. I guess I'm stupid but I'd been hoping it would take months, or that maybe I'd go all school year and never see him at all.

Is it too much to hope that the universe makes his parents decide to move them out of the state?

I can't believe he moved on so quickly, and with someone so much prettier and shorter than me. I mean, I know we only dated two months but I thought it was going well. We never fought. I let him hang out with his guy friends and I didn't whine about it because I know guys hate that. I wasn't clingy, and I didn't make him take me to expensive places on dates. I was the perfect girlfriend.

And all of that means nothing, because I know what caused this relationship to fail. Me.

Big, tall, awkward, me.

I take a deep breath and throw the covers off. I stare at the ceiling and try to just fall the hell asleep like a normal person. But I can't stop thinking about it. Honestly, all summer long was just like this. I'd throw myself into working on that greenhouse, and I'd feel better, but then bedtime comes around and suddenly I can't sleep.

I don't exactly miss Shawn so much as I miss what having a boyfriend feels like. It was easy falling asleep when we were dating. I'd lay right here in this same bed, but I'd have my phone. He'd Snap me a goofy photo and send bitmoji's telling me goodnight.

I'd send them back. He'd send hearts and kissy faces.

I fell asleep every night those two months feeling like someone cared about me. Now I just lay here, hating myself for being tall. Hating guys for being shallow. Hating every short girl on earth.

It's only the second day of school and yet it feels like I've been doing this for decades. Like waking up and dragging my ass to the bus stop is the worst sort of torture ever. It's all because I know once I get to school, I might run into Shawn and his new girlfriend. And if I do, I'll put on a smiling face, I'll seem happy and normal, and like I don't even care.

And it's all just so stupid I want to scream.

Livi meets me outside as soon as the bus arrives at school and hands me a cup of coffee. "Good morning," she singsongs as her golden hair flows around her shoulders. It's somehow even shiner today, and I'm betting that's on purpose.

I take the coffee and give her a wary look. "Why are you so happy?"

She shrugs quickly and takes a sip of her coffee. "I'm

trying this *fake it till you make it* thing. If I act like I love school, then maybe I eventually will."

I snort. "Good luck with that. And thanks for the coffee."

"Only one hundred and eighty one days left of this bullshit," Livi says as we step to the side. A group of ROTC guys are carrying a large cafeteria table outside for whatever reason.

"School just started and you're already counting down the days?" I say with a laugh.

"Yep. Don't underestimate the power of positive thinking. One day you'll step off the bus and I'll be like, 'only one more day!' and you'll say, 'wow, this year went by fast'."

I roll my eyes. "Can that day hurry up and get here?"

Now we can't even get into the school because more guys are carrying more tables out of the side entrance. Livi and I step off the sidewalk and onto the grass to wait for them to pass.

This is a bad thing, because my eyes wander to the parking lot, and I know I should stop them, but I don't. I go straight for that part of the back row where he always parked his truck. Sure enough, Shawn's truck is there, parked next to a shiny red BMW. I see Mindy climb out of her car and walk over to his truck.

My heart aches and my head tells me it's all my fault for being so grossly tall that no guy can find me attractive. I force myself to look away.

And that's when I see my greenhouse.

"Oh my God." I'm not sure if I actually say the words or just think them, because I'm in shock. I can't stop staring at it.

"What?" Livi says. A moment later she says, "Oh shit. What happened?"

At first, I think maybe the wind knocked it down. Maybe I didn't build it as strongly as I thought I did. Maybe this is all my fault. But then, I notice the holes dotting the one back wall that's still remaining standing. Nature doesn't cause destruction like that. Humans do.

Someone destroyed my greenhouse.

CHAPTER FOUR

GAVIN

WHEN I WAKE UP, my head is pounding. My mouth tastes like death, and the sunlight peering in my window feels like a laser blasting through my eyeballs and scaring my brain.

Shit.

I push myself up and realize I fell asleep on top of the sheets last night. I'm still wearing the same thing I was wearing after school yesterday. My brain is foggy, my head feels like someone keeps hitting it with a hammer. I am officially hung over.

How the hell did this happen?

I drag myself off the bed and get in the shower. I only have about twenty minutes before I need to be at school, so I make it quick. The cold water wakes me up, but my head is still pounding as memories of last night come back to me. Dad getting the cops called on him, me going out with the guys.

It was TJ, that prick. After we blew apart that greenhouse, I still had anger inside of me, roiling around being pissed at my dad. So he offered me a drink from the bottle of tequila he kept in his backpack.

I let my head lean against the shower wall as I slowly remember what happened last night. I got drunk as hell in my own driveway. After dropping off TJ at his house, I came home and drank while sitting on the tailgate of my truck and looking up at the stars. I don't remember finally going to bed, but the empty bottle of tequila on my floor isn't a good sign.

Fear grips me. This is not the man I want to be. I get dressed and brush my teeth and down some aspirin and all the while I'm thinking it to myself, on repeat.

I'm turning into my worthless father.

I know I can't stay home sick on the second day of school. The school would call my parents and my dad would find out and he'd blast me a new one. I have to somehow make it through this day even though I feel like total shit.

At least one good thing is happening this morning. Dad isn't home when I walk into the living room. He started a new roofing job today and probably left the house around five in the morning.

Mom is in the kitchen, still dressed in her khaki pants and dark blue Walmart shirt. "Want some pancakes?" she says. She offers me a smile too, but her eyes are weary and I know she just wants to go to bed. But she's standing at the stove, making breakfast for me, which is dinner for her, just like she does every day.

"Sure," I say, grabbing a plate and slinking to the table. I chug a cup of water and then refill it two more times. I'll be pissing like crazy in first period, but the faster this alcohol gets out of my system, the better.

Once I'm sober again, I can start thinking clearly and

telling myself to stop drinking. Stop going out with those guys. Stop doing shit I'll regret in the morning.

But I have to admit that tearing down that greenhouse was exhilarating. I wasn't even drunk then, which is good because it means I can still feel alive without being numbed by alcohol.

I tell myself I'll never be like my dad, but on days when I wake up hung over, I really start to question that.

Mom is so tired that she eats across from me at the table and doesn't say anything. I don't talk, either. Sometimes just sitting in the silence that appears when Dad is gone is all we need.

I drink some more water, and make myself walk in a straight line down the tile grout in the kitchen. I'm fine. No longer drunk, just hungover.

I drive to school, hoping this day will go by quickly so I can get home and sleep. And then I remember that I work tonight, so sleep won't happen. Monday, Wednesday, Friday is soccer practice after school. Tuesdays and Thursdays are when I work at Magic Mark's Pizza. I get there right after school and then deliver pizzas until midnight. Once again, I tell myself I'm the biggest idiot ever for getting wasted on a school *and* work night.

Then I haul my worthless ass out of the truck and walk into school five minutes after the bell rings.

I slink into homeroom, and the teacher gives me the stink eye from where she stands at the front of the class. I don't even try to come up with an excuse for my tardiness. I just walk to my seat and slide in behind that girl from yesterday. She smells like strawberries, which is a nice change from the rest of the school that smells like teen angst, body odor, and cheap cleaning chemicals.

I slouch in my chair, happy that the aspirin has helped a little bit, and pretend to listen to the announcements on the PA system.

TJ whispers my name and I look over at him. "You look like shit."

I shrug.

He snorts and shakes his head. "You got no self-control, dude."

I know he's talking about the alcohol and how he probably knows I finished off the bottle after he went home. I want to tell him he has no self-control, either. If he's not punching holes in the walls at home, he's finding random shit to destroy, like that stupid greenhouse. We all have our vices.

I wish mine was a little better.

I glance back at Beau, who is sleeping on his desk, and wish I could do the same thing, but I can't sleep in class. I've never been able to let my guard down like that.

When the announcements are over, our incredibly old homeroom teacher passes out papers. It's some kind of flyer for volunteer work, another one advertising school spirit shirts for sale. Just crap that means nothing to me. I shove it in my backpack and watch the girl in front of me.

She seems off today. Yesterday she was all straight-backed and paying attention, being a perfect student. Today her shoulders slump, and I don't think she lifts her cheek off her hand at all. She just sits there staring at her desk.

I don't know why I care, but I want to know what's up with her. Why she's being all blah today.

I lean forward and tap her on the shoulder. She turns

around slowly, leveling an evil glare at me. "What?" she mouths.

I shrug. "You okay?"

I actually said the words instead of mouthing them, but she stares at me like she didn't hear me at first. Then she turns back around.

I tap her shoulder again, realizing how not used to this I am. Most girls talk to me even when I don't want them to. "Leave me alone," she mutters.

I lean forward, breathing in the scent of her strawberry shampoo. "You just seem pissed, so I was curious."

She turns slightly toward me, so that I can see the curve of her lips and smell the coffee she drank earlier. "We aren't friends," she says softly before turning back to face the front.

"No talking!" the teacher barks.

"Dude," TJ says a moment later. He points to his phone, where someone just texted him. "There's two cop cars out back."

I glance over and see the picture on his phone. Sure enough, there are two police cars parked in the teacher's lot. The lot next to the edge of the property. Right where that greenhouse used to be.

I stiffen. TJ's got this smirk on his face like he's impressed that he caused something worthy of police attention. But I'm not so cocky. There's no way they can trace that back to us, right? And who even cares about the damage, because it was just a stupid greenhouse that's been there forever. They can't possibly care about that. They're probably here for something else.

I look over at TJ and he shrugs, like it's no big deal. So I decide he's right. No big deal. This won't come back to us.

And then the door opens and our principal walks into the classroom. My stomach tightens, and I suddenly feel like I'm going to puke.

He talks quietly to the teacher and then they both turn and look directly at me.

"Clarissa?" the principal says, waving his hand for her to join him.

The girl in front of me stands up, slinging her backpack on her shoulder. She must be Clarissa, I realize, as relief rolls over me. The principal wasn't looking at me, he was looking at her. This has nothing to do with the cops. Nothing to do with the greenhouse.

Everything is fine.

CHAPTER FIVE

Clarissa

I'VE NEVER BEEN CALLED to the principal's office. In fact, I'm pretty sure I've never even talked with the man in all my time of being at this high school. Still, I'm nervous as hell when I'm called to the front of the class, even though I know I haven't done anything wrong. Maybe there's something wrong with my schedule. Hopefully it's not some kind of emergency.

"Hi, Clarissa," he says as we step out of the classroom and the heavy door swings shut behind us.

"Hello..." I say, as my thoughts shoot off in different directions. Why is the principal walking with me? Even knowing I haven't done anything wrong, I'm still a little scared right now.

"I'd like you to join me in my office with Linda Bradley," he continues, his steps much longer than mine so I have to rush to keep up with him.

"Mrs. Bradley?" I say, totally confused. But then I remember what I saw this morning, and I'm pretty sure I know why the boss of my part time job is here at the school. "Is this about the greenhouse?"

"Yes. I'm afraid some vandals have destroyed it. Linda Bradley asked me to get you because I hear you've had something to do with maintaining it."

I shrug. "I built it this summer. We were supposed to plant flowers in it for the kids."

"That's a shame," he says as we step into the front office. He leads me down the hallway and to his office, which is huge and has a whole wall of windows that faces the front of the school.

Mrs. Bradley sits in one of the chairs, and she smiles at me as I enter. "Have you seen the damage?" she asks. Little frown lines cross her forehead.

I nod. "I saw it from a distance this morning, but I haven't been over there yet. What happened?"

"I'm afraid it was vandalized," Principal Walsh says. "The police have already looked into it, and I've asked for more time to find the culprits before they do anything."

"Oh, I don't want to press charges," Mrs. Bradley says, shaking her head. A strand of her auburn hair falls out of the bun on top of her head. "I would like restitution so we can buy the materials and rebuild."

She looks over at me, giving me this encouraging smile that I guess is supposed to make me feel better.

"Is any of it salvageable?" I ask.

They both shake their head. "I'm afraid the damage was extensive," says Principal Walsh.

My throat tightens. No, no, no, Clarissa. Don't do this here, my brain screams. But my heart doesn't listen, and soon hot tears are pouring from my eyes, rolling down my cheeks.

I swipe them away as soon as they begin, but it's no use. I keep thinking of the greenhouse, of all that hard work and sweat and blood I poured into it with Grandpa. Mrs. Bradley's hand rubs my back.

"It's all right, sweetheart," she says. "We'll fix it."

I shake my head. "I can't fix it. Not without my grandpa."

When I look up, both the principal and Mrs. Bradley are watching me with curious expressions. I take a deep breath and explain. "He has glaucoma. He did all the hard work this summer but now he's mostly blind. He can't help me build it again."

"We can hire someone," Mrs. Bradley says. "It's okay. We'll get someone to build it."

I shake my head. "It's not the same. I was doing this for my grandmother and now it's just—not the same."

I look at my hands in my lap and try to remember all the work Grandpa did this summer. Building the wooden frame and raising it into place was the hardest part. Maybe Livi can help me and we can do it again. I'll need tools and more strength than I have, though.

The office door opens and a short woman with curly black hair enters. "I found something," she says, handing Principal Walsh a flash drive. "I believe you were right."

"So it *was* a student who did this?" he says, frown lines deepening on his lips. He shakes his head. "Since the property lines are so close together, we've had trouble with students going to the daycare over the years. Usually they just hop the fence and play on the playground after hours. But this is unacceptable and not at all the kind of behavior I'd expect from a Sweets High student."

He plugs in the flash drive and then turns his computer monitor sideways so we can all see it.

The video is of security footage from the side of the school building. It's black and white, in night vision mode, and the picture isn't that clear, but I can make out my greenhouse in the distance. It's still standing when the video starts.

We all watch silently as a guy runs up to it. He's swaying a little like he might be drunk. He turns around and yells in the distance. Then another guy runs up. They seem to argue for a minute, but we can't hear anything because the video doesn't have any sound.

I watch the two figures as one of them picks up a hammer, my hammer, and swings it at my beautiful greenhouse.

My heart plummets as the first hole cracks through the surface. The drunk guy throws his hands in the air victoriously and swings some more. It almost seems like the second guy is trying to talk him out of it, but before long, he's taken up another tool and is smashing my greenhouse, too.

My chest aches and I want to look away.

"I'm sickened to say that these people are definitely high school students," Principal Walsh says.

"Wow," Mrs. Bradley murmurs as we watch the guys swing together at one of the corner posts. It wobbles and shakes, but eventually it falls, taking half the roof with it.

My tears have dried up, but it hurts so bad to watch these assholes rip apart my entire summer's work. They jump on the green plastic walls, cracking them into bits so they can never be used again. My clay pots are thrown and smashed. The five gallon bucket Grandpa used as a chair gets slammed against the concrete foundation until it cracks in half.

"What is wrong with people?" I say softly as I continue to watch the destruction.

"Maybe they will get closer to the camera when they leave," Principal Walsh says. "We need to find a way to identify them."

We keep watching the destruction on screen. It lasts for over twenty minutes. When my entire greenhouse is destroyed, the two people stop and admire their work. They look like guys, but from the small, grainy video footage, it's hard to tell for sure.

When they decide to leave the scene, they don't come closer to the school like we'd hoped. Instead they just walk the property line between the daycare and the school and head back to the road. But right before they leave the camera's pathway, they walk under the light of a nearby streetlamp.

The light illuminates the bright white logo on the front of their matching black hoodies.

The Hornets Soccer team logo.

Only a handful of students in this entire school have that jacket. They are all guys, and they're all on the soccer team.

"It should be easy to weed out who is responsible for this," Principal Walsh says. "And when we do, we will get restitution for you, Linda."

Mrs. Bradley nods, then turns her attention to me. "It'll be okay, Clarissa. We'll get the greenhouse fixed again. I know how important it is to you."

I nod dumbly but I'm not really paying attention. All I can think about is the memory of that video, of those complete jerks who would destroy something that's not theirs. I think of the soccer team hoodies, how all of those popular jocks walk around wearing it all day long.

And then I think of my homeroom class where I sit next to three of them. They're always loud and obnoxious, making jokes and whispering stupid stuff to each other when we're supposed to be paying attention in class. Like Gavin Voss, who has a face that's permanently cocky, and he's so stuck up he thinks it's okay to put his feet on someone else's chair.

I don't know which one of these guys destroyed my grandpa's last project, but as soon as I find out, I will make them pay.

CHAPTER SIX

GAVIN

I'M bored to death in second period AP Chemistry when the speaker beeps with an announcement. My teacher sighs and lowers his dry erase marker from where he'd been writing equations on the board. This all boring stuff we learned last year, so I haven't been taking notes.

Above us, the principal's voice rings out through the speaker.

"Attention Sweets High School students. It has come to my attention that two of you participated in the vandalism of a greenhouse that belongs to Little Lone Stars Daycare next door."

What? That old building didn't belong to the school?

He continues, "I am asking the persons responsible to come forward immediately. If you know any information that will lead to finding the culprits, please come forward. Tips can be made anonymously through the school's website under the link that says contact us. I hope everyone understands that when one student does something terrible, it reflects badly on all of us. Please come forward immediately. Thank you."

I chew on the inside of my lip until it bleeds. My teacher turns back to the board and keeps writing his equations. I glance around the classroom and no one seems to care about what we just heard. This is an AP class, so it's full of smart people who usually never do anything wrong. Do they all assume someone else did it? That no one in this room is capable of mindless destruction?

I tap my pen rapidly against the desk. I can't believe that thing belonged to the daycare. The idea of destroying a piece of school property is kind of hilarious, especially one that's not in use. But now that I know it wasn't even on our campus, I feel like shit.

A new type of fear slivers its way up my spine when I think of what would happen to me at home if my parents found out what I did. My dad is hard enough to deal with on a day when he's not pissed at the world. My palms go sweaty at the very thought of him finding out the truth.

I shake my head and roll my shoulders, telling myself to get it together.

I don't know why they made that announcement. They clearly don't know who did it, so it could be anyone. Someone who doesn't go to school anymore, or even a total stranger just passing through town. I take a deep breath and tell myself to chill out. They won't find out that it was me and TJ. They just won't.

After class, TJ practically slams into me in the hallway. His eyes are wide. "Dude, you keep your mouth shut."

"About what?" I say, shoving him off me as we walk to our third period class.

"You know what," he hisses.

"Dude, shut up. Just don't even talk about it. No one will find out."

He shoves me on the arm. "You better not crack and go narc on me."

"Why would I tell on you?" I say in a hushed voice. "I'd be telling on myself too, you dumbass. My lips are sealed."

TJ nods once, his jaw tight. "Good."

I've pretty much forgotten the whole thing until seventh period athletics. As soon as I hit the locker room and change into my practice soccer uniform, I realize the loud rock music isn't playing like it normally is from Coach's office.

As we file out of the locker room and onto the field, Coach tells us to stand in line in front of the bleachers.

"Have a seat," he says. He seems pissed, which is odd because Coach is usually laid back and fun. Two people down, TJ is glaring at me and I have no idea why.

"You know where I just came from?" Coach asks, but it's in that way where we know he doesn't want us to answer. "A meeting with the police and the school administration. I spent an hour watching a security video, trying to figure out which of my athletes were the two men responsible for vandalizing a small business' greenhouse."

I nearly crap myself on the spot. I don't dare look over at TJ so I don't give us away. Coach is taking turns staring us all down. I lift my eyebrows like I'm totally shocked to hear this news, like I can't believe one of my teammates did something so stupid.

"Next time you decide to commit a crime, make sure you're not on a security camera, and make damn sure you're not wearing the Hornet's soccer hoodie."

He paces the length of the bleachers where the fourteen of us are sitting. "I was so proud of my varsity team this summer when we were doing training. And now, on the first day of school, you've gone and ruined our reputation."

"Not all of us!" Mickey Russo says. "You said it was two people! You can't blame this on all of us!"

Coach whirls on him. "This is a team. What one of you does reflects on all of you." He turns back to face us, his eyes narrowed. "Two of you are guilty and I hope you both come forward. I'll give you thirty seconds to be honorable and do it now."

He goes silent and we all sit here. My heart is pounding, but I know he doesn't know who actually did it or he would have taken us to the principal already. I casually glance down and then look slightly to my left. TJ is looking straight at me. I look away.

The thirty seconds seems to take forever. No one says a word. No one does anything.

Eventually, Coach looks at his watch and then back at us. "I'm very disappointed. Get up and hit the field. We'll be doing drills all day today."

A chorus of groans echoes what I'm thinking. Drills are hardcore workouts. Burpees, pushups, sprints. They suck.

Coach waves his hand to shut us up. "Until the two people responsible for the vandalism fess up, you'll be doing drills every practice. I'm tempted to forfeit all of our games as well."

"Turn yourself in," Mickey yells, glowering at his teammates.

"Yeah!" someone else says.

I nod like an idiot, like I agree with them. The guilty person should just turn themselves in.

I've never felt more stupid in my life.

We hit the field and do drills until my chest aches and my leg muscles are screaming. Everyone bitches about it, and the guys keep telling each other to just turn yourself in if you did the vandalism. Carlos Valdes even makes a stand at one point, saying how do we know those hoodies in the video are even real, or that two other people, maybe players from our rival team didn't steal our hoodies to commit this crime on purpose.

I have to admit, I get behind that one. We all talk it out while doing the drills, coming up with scenarios where maybe the hoodies were faked, made with a homemade screen printing machine for the sole purpose of malice.

Coach doesn't care about any of our theories, though. He just makes us do drills until our two hours is over and we all feel like we're going to die.

I hit the locker room and shower quickly. All I want to do is get home and take another shower, one with actual hot water, and then down some pain meds to soothe my aching muscles. I thought I was in pretty good shape before today. But doing two hours of drills really wears you out.

The locker room is quieter than usual as we pack up to head home. It's like everyone is suspicious of everyone else. We're all looking for someone to blame for the extra drill punishment we all had to endure. I keep to myself, knowing the blame lies solely with TJ and me, and feeling like absolute shit for it.

But there's no way I can turn myself in now. My dad would kill me. The team would hate me. TJ would be pissed. Not to mention, it would be embarrassing as hell.

I grab my keys and head out to the parking lot, realizing I'm one of the last guys to leave. I guess everyone else was so pissed and exhausted that they rushed home. I walk slowly, my legs still aching, making my way out to my truck which is parked on the last row. Now I wish I hadn't gotten to school late today so I could have parked closer and saved myself this agonizing walk.

I glance over at the destroyed greenhouse as I pass it, noting that it's totally in the boundaries of the daycare's property. How had I not noticed that before? The grass is even a little greener over there because they have a sprinkler system installed.

I nearly trip over my own feet when I see someone sitting there, at the heap of rubble that used to be a greenhouse.

She's folded her knees up to her chest, and her chin rests on top of them. I recognize her hair first. It's the girl from my homeroom class. Clarissa something.

I get into my truck and watch her. I wonder if she needs a ride home. There's only two cars left in the parking lot, mine and Coach's. But she's just sitting there, not looking like she's in a hurry to leave.

Why would anyone want to sit by an old greenhouse?

She lifts her head and uses both of her hands to wipe under her eyes. Is she crying?

Over a stupid greenhouse?

I bite on my lip. I don't even know this girl but now I'm

dying to ask her what she's doing, mourning the loss of something that belongs to a daycare. But just like earlier today when I could have come clean, I don't do what I should do. If the way that girl treats me in class is any indication, she doesn't want me poking around in her life trying to ask what's wrong. So I let it go, start my truck and drive away.

CHAPTER SEVEN

Clarissa

"YOU CAN'T GO wrong with a good vegetable," Grandpa says. "Something kids like to eat, like maybe green peas or even sunflowers where they can eat the seeds."

He feels for his coffee cup on the end table and then gently lifts it to his face, feeling the rim of the mug so he knows where to drink from. "Just don't do tomatoes. Kids hate tomatoes."

"That's a good idea," I say. I'm sitting next to him on the couch, picking at a bowl of cereal for dinner. It's been four days since my greenhouse was destroyed, and I still haven't found the strength to tell Grandpa about it. I'm starting to think I just won't say anything.

His going blind is the worst thing ever, but at least now he'll never drive past the daycare and see for himself that I've lied. Plus, I tell myself I'm only lying to make him feel better. He'd be devastated if he knew the truth. This greenhouse is his last project ever.

This past weekend I did basically nothing but sit around and feel sorry for myself. I worked at the daycare on Friday after school, and I kept the kids busy with a movie. Only a couple of them asked about the greenhouse, which I'd promised would be ready when school started, and I told them I still needed a few days.

But really, I have no idea what to do. Mrs. Bradley told the principal she'd accept reimbursement for the cost of our materials that were destroyed. She said if I can't rebuild it myself, we can either decide to scrap the project all together, or she can have the school pay for the cost of hiring someone else to build it. Right now, we're in limbo.

The principal vows that he'll find the two students responsible for the damage, but until then, we're not really doing much of anything.

I want to build the greenhouse back. I want it back. I want to make the kids happy and I want to see my Grandma's legacy go on for another generation. I'd also like to stop lying to Grandpa. Once it's built back, then I can tell him the truth about what we're planting each month. I can share true stories about the kids at the daycare instead of making them up.

But I know I can't build that thing by myself, and hiring a contractor just seems so wrong. This greenhouse was built my hand, not by a professional. I want it to have that rustic handmade look.

At night, I do fifty pushups before bed, telling myself that I can be strong enough to do this alone. I can't give up on my greenhouse, or my kids at the daycare. I made them a promise, and I will see it through.

On Tuesday morning, I walk into class exhausted from yet another night of fitful sleep. I can't stop replaying that security camera video in my head. I can't stop seeing those two assholes smashing up my creation. In my dreams, the faces turn closer to the camera, and suddenly come into focus. But every time when I'm about to see who it is, I'll burst awake and the dream will be gone.

I heave a sigh and walk to my desk in homeroom.

The three soccer players are chatting like they do every morning until Mrs. Lin shuts them up. And like usual, they're all wearing those stupid hoodies.

Although, unlike usual, I decide not to ignore them. "Good morning," I say, making the barest eye contact with Gavin Voss before I slide into my seat.

"Ice Queen talks," one of his idiot friends says from the next row over.

Normally, I'd ignore him, but since I'm trying something new, I turn and give him a smile.

"Sometimes."

"Sometimes you talk, or sometimes you're an ice queen?" he says. He's shorter than Gavin, with a dark tan and shaggy black hair. I think his name is TJ, but I'm never sure with the jocks because I'm not friends with any of them.

I shrug, and try for a coy smile. "Both."

Then I turn back around. Baby steps. If I want to trick these guys into thinking I'm their friend, I'll need to be casual about it. Maybe if I can win one of them over, they'll tell me who destroyed my greenhouse. They're a team, after all. I'm sure they all know exactly who did it.

Maybe if I can get one of them to crack...

A few seconds later, there's a tap on my shoulder. I glance to my right, smelling his cologne before I see him.

I lift an eyebrow.

Gavin Voss leans forward, his face just inches from mine. "I thought you hated me," he whispers.

I lift one shoulder in a shrug. "Hate is a strong word."

"Sorry I had my feet on your desk."

I hear his chair squeak as he sits back in his desk. I swallow. Here I was thinking these jocks are total assholes, but maybe some of them are okay. He did apologize after all.

Mrs. Lin shushes everyone when the announcements come on the speaker and I sit here trying to focus, but I can't stop thinking of that smell of his cologne. It's like the woods and leather all mixed into one. It makes me want to smell it again.

Fifteen minutes later, the bell rings, and I rise from my chair, sliding my backpack over my shoulders. Gavin stands too, and the only thing I can think for a whole ten seconds is that this boy is taller than me. By about three or four inches, too.

He looks me right in the eyes, his brown hair glinting under the florescent lights. His forearm flexes as he holds onto his backpack strap.

Get it together, Clarissa.

I exhale. "Have a nice day, boys." I smile and glance at the other two soccer players so it doesn't seem like I'm *just* talking to Gavin.

"You too, Ice Queen," TJ says, nodding at me. The other guy who sits behind him, is a little stocky for a soccer player. I give him a quick look before turning to leave, and I mentally cross him off my list. The two guys on the video were tall and thin. That guy is too short and thick to be one of the culprits.

He's off my shit list for now.

But the rest of the soccer players are all suspects, including the gorgeous Gavin Voss.

Oh my God, Clarissa, don't call him gorgeous.

"Hey," Gavin says right as he appears by my side as we step into the hallway. "I have AP History next. What about you?"

"Math," I say, glancing over at him as we walk. Actually… I have to glance *up* a little bit. This guy is one of the rare guys who are taller than I am. "You're in AP history?"

"What? You think I'm too stupid for AP classes?"

His lazy grin stretches wider. I notice that his lips are a shade of pink I've never seen before. His eyes are blue, like a swimming pool, and it's hard to look away.

I shrug. "I didn't say that."

"But you thought it."

"No, I didn't."

The truth is, I did. I guess I have such a bad impression of the soccer players that I assume they're all as stupid as the balls they kick around.

"I'm in all AP classes," he says, dodging a group of students in the way. When it does, his arm brushes against mine and sends tingles down my spine. Walking with a guy reminds me of when I dated Shawn. We were only together the last month of school, but it was glorious having someone to walk to class with you. Now, it almost feels the same way again.

"Well, I'm not in any AP classes," I say with a sigh. "I'm as average as it gets." I blink. "Well, except for—" but then I shut the hell up. I can't believe I almost spilled my biggest embarrassment—how tall I am.

Gavin doesn't seem to notice or care. His smile is a thousand times more sincere than the sneer he gave me on that first day of school. "If you ever need a tutor, let me know."

I don't say anything as I turn down the math hallway. He'd said he'd had history next, which is all the way across the school. So why is he still walking with me?

I look over at him and find that he's watching me, too.

"Hey, um, it's Clarissa, right?" He actually seems nervous.

"Yes."

"Cool. So, Clarissa," he says, scratching the back of his neck. "I think I saw you the other day after school. You were sitting on the grass between the school and the daycare next door?"

I bite down on my lip. When the hell did he see me? I thought I was alone. And I definitely did some crying that day, so even though I try to act calm, I can feel heat rising in my cheeks.

But maybe this can be the first way I try to crack away at the soccer team, gaining their trust to find out who ruined my greenhouse.

I shrug. "There was this greenhouse there, and someone smashed it."

I study him carefully, waiting for those blue eyes of his to give away that he knows something about it. He just blinks.

"Why would someone smash it?" he asks.

I shrug. "I don't know, but I work at that daycare so it really pissed me off."

"I see."

I take a deep breath and lower my voice so I don't seem pissed off. "I just wish I knew who did it, you know?" I have no idea where I'm going with this, and being a sneaky spy has never been my strong point. So I think fast and come up with something that might make him tell me what he knows. "I just really want to know who did it and why, because now I'm worried that, like, someone targeted me or something."

His eyes widen. "Why would someone target you?"

I shrug and try to look pitiful. "I don't know, but it was kind of *my* greenhouse, so I worry that maybe someone hates me and they did it on purpose."

He shakes his head. "No, that's not what happened."

My heartbeat quickens. Is this it? Is he going to tell me what he knows about his teammates? "How do you know?"

He shrugs just as the tardy bell rings. "You just seem like a nice person, so I'm sure no one did it to hurt you."

CHAPTER EIGHT

GAVIN

DAD'S ON A RAMPAGE. I'm doing my best to ignore him. It's after nine at night and I'm lying in bed, my earbuds in while I listen to music. But Dad's deep, angry voice reverberates through the walls, and although I can't tell what he's ranting about, I know he's still yelling.

Mom is home too, because it's her day off work, and I really hate that he's ruining it by being an ass. But she's not yelling back, so I don't think he's mad at her. He's probably just mad at the world, like always.

Another half an hour goes by and I'm still trying to ignore it, but even the loudest music I've got doesn't drown out the sound. I am so freaking exhausted from endless drills at soccer practice and then delivering pizzas on my days off. I just want to sleep.

I want to stop fearing that at any minute, I'll be caught for what I did. I'm sure it'll blow over, but Coach sure isn't making it easy on us.

I turn off my music and walk to my door, listening to see exactly what it is that has my dad all pissed off. But now he's no longer yelling, and has instead decided to stomp through the kitchen and to the living room.

I open my door a crack and stick my head out. From my room, I can see down the hallway and partly into the kitchen. Mom is sitting at the table, using her old laptop that tends to freeze up more than it works. For Christmas, I hope to buy her a new one. The glow of the screen highlights the dark circles under her eyes.

"I found a shop that will do a free estimate," she calls out to my dad.

A few seconds later, he storms into the kitchen. "I don't need an estimate. I know what's wrong with it. The brakes don't work."

"Maybe they could tell you if it'll really cost that much money," Mom says, her voice soft. It's the soothing tone she takes when he's trying to calm him down.

"Doesn't matter what it costs!" he shouts. Guess her calm voice didn't help. Dad takes a long sip from his beer bottle. "It's still a few hundred dollars at best. We don't have that."

I step into the hallway and the hardwood floor creaks beneath me. Both of my parents turn to look at me, Mom with her soft eyes and Dad with his glassy ones.

"The brakes went out on my truck," Dad says without me needing to ask. "I damn near died on the highway today."

"Wow, that sucks."

Dad looks at me like I'm stupid. "You think?"

"What will it cost to fix?"

"Three hundred," Mom says, which I barely hear because Dad talks over her.

"Too freaking much, that's how much. I don't have cash

just lying around after I spend it all on this house and these bills."

I know what happens if Dad can't drive his own car to work every day. He'll take mine.

And while I'm happy to help out, that's just not going to work. I've poured my soul into my 2004 Chevy pickup truck and I'm not going to let him drive it the way he drives his.

I slip into my bedroom and pull open my sock drawer, taking out three hundred dollar bills from the envelope I stash under my boxers. When I go back to the kitchen, my parents are once again arguing as if I'd never been there just thirty seconds before. It's giving me a headache.

"Here," I say, tossing the cash to the table. "Get your brakes fixed."

"What the hell is this?" Dad says, taking the money and staring at it as if he's never seen such a thing. "You a drug dealer or something?"

"I have a job, Dad. I worked all summer and saved up."

His eyes narrow. "How much cash do you have?"

"Not much more than that," I lie. "But I want you to have it. Mom and I need you to be able to get to work." It never hurts to stroke his ego, and plus, it's true. Without Dad's job, we'd be screwed.

Dad puts the cash in his back pocket. Mom gives me this quick look, thanking me with her eyes. I smile at her.

For just the slightest moment, it looks like Dad might actually thank me. But then he scowls. "Don't expect to be paid back, boy. If anything, *you* owe *me* much more than this for putting a roof over your head and feeding you all these years."

I could argue that taking care of your own child is kind of

what the law requires and that he's not a saint for it, but I don't. I just nod because I'm exhausted and just want the damn yelling to stop. "Understood."

Back in my room, I don't need my earbuds anymore because Dad is finally content. I go to my sock drawer and pull out the envelope of cash, knowing that it needs a better hiding spot now that my dad knows I have some money. I look around my room, and finally settle on pulling up the corner of the carpet that's under my bed. I shove the money under there and then toss some dirty clothes on top of it.

Then, just for good measure, I take out a few twenties and put it back in my sock drawer. If Dad goes snooping for my money, I want him to think he found it.

When I slam the drawer closed, it rattles, reminding me that there's half a bottle of whiskey in there from a party I went to over the summer. I open the drawer again, and grab the bottle from the back of it. The amber liquid sloshes around, practically begging me to take a long sip. Just enough to calm my stress and lull me to sleep.

But then just as quickly, a sickening feeling falls over me. I feel slimy thinking this way. That's what my dad does. He drinks to forget about all of his pathetic problems. If I did the same, I'd be no better off than him.

And I have to be better than him.

I put the bottle back in the drawer. I am not my dad.

A tiny voice in the back of my head whispers that my dad also wouldn't confess to vandalism. I tell it to shut up.

The next morning, I find myself rushing to school for possibly the stupidest reason ever. Those first fifteen minutes of class. The rest of the school day is boring and filled with AP classwork, but those first fifteen minutes are the most interesting minutes of my day.

Even though I'm here five minutes before the bell rings, Clarissa is already in her seat in homeroom, along with a couple of other students who'd rather sit in a desk than socialize in the hallways.

"Good morning," I say, grinning at her as I walk by. She's wearing a V-neck shirt that's not exactly low cut, but it shows enough skin to make me wonder how soft it'd feel to run my lips across her collarbone. Her hair is always shiny and straight, which makes me want to run my fingers through it.

I'm finding that I want to do a lot of things where Clarissa is concerned.

"Morning," she says, lifting an eyebrow as I slip into my desk. "Did you see the good news?"

"What's that?" I ask, leaning forward slightly. She's turned sideways so we can talk, and I want to do whatever it takes to keep her this way. The back of her head is pretty, but the front of her is better.

She nods her head and I follow the direction to see a much younger, much shorter woman behind the teacher's desk. "Who's that?" I whisper.

"Substitute," she whispers back, giving me a grin. "I remember her from last year. She lets you do whatever you want."

"Nice." I bite my lip. I'm running out of things to talk about, but I don't want to stop talking. "Homeroom is supposed to be a blow off class anyway."

She rolls her eyes. "It's supposed to be a class to get important information."

"Same thing."

She gives me a look that makes my heart skip a beat.

The guys walk in just as the bell rings, and they're both absorbed with TJ's phone.

"Dude," TJ says as he slides into the seat to the left of mine. "The cheerleading sleepover is all over Snapchat. You want in?"

He tips his phone toward me, showing a snap of three girls in their underwear having a pillow fight. Normally I'd be all over this. But Clarissa is within earshot and I want to make a good impression. "You know they post that shit just for attention, right?"

"Yeah, *duh*," Beau says. "That's what makes it so good."

I open my binder as if there's something important in there. TJ snorts. "He just wants to look at them at home where he has some privacy."

"Dude," I say. "Shut the hell up."

"Ugh, such a teacher's pet these days," TJ says, which makes absolutely no sense, but whatever.

"He's just pissed about the soccer drills," Beau says. "We're all pissy about that."

"Punishing the whole team for something one of us did is stupid."

TJ looks at me for a long moment and in the corner of my eyes, I see Clarissa turn slightly toward us. She's listening.

"They said it was two people," I say, playing this game with TJ where we act like we're innocent. "And yeah, I'm sick of the drills. Someone needs to fess up already."

Now Clarissa turns all the way toward us. She widens

her eyes like she's sharing a secret. "Do you know who did it? Was it one of the hot ones?"

"Whoa," TJ says, putting a hand to his chest. "Are you saying I'm not one of the hot soccer players?"

"No, but..." She stumbles over her words and I'm ninety-nine percent sure she's lying. "My friends think it's that super hot guy on the team, because he seems like a rule breaker." She shrugs. "I don't really care, but they'd freak out if it was him."

"Who exactly is this really hot guy?" I ask, both because I think she's lying in an effort to find out who ruined the greenhouse, and because up until now, I've always felt like I'm on the more attractive side when it comes to my teammates.

Hey, I'm not trying to be an arrogant asshole here. It just is what it is.

"I don't know his name," she says, not meeting my eyes. "He's tall. Brown hair, I think."

"Dude, she's describing you," Beau says, smacking me on the arm.

Clarissa turns bright red, which is probably the cutest thing ever. She covers it by rolling her eyes. "I said super hot, not super cocky."

I lean back in my chair, fixing her with my favorite smirk. "I see how it is."

Beau and TJ go back to looking at Snapchat and Clarissa turns back around. I spend the rest of homeroom trying to think of something to talk about, but I'm speechless. This has never happened with girls before.

Maybe I'm just out of practice. I stopped dating midway through last school year because my home life was just too crazy. Between soccer games, working at Magic Mark's, and dealing with my embarrassment of a father, it's hard trying to keep up with a girl.

And I know from experience that they get pissed if you're not able to hang out with them all the time. So why the hell am I sitting here thinking about this girl in front of me? Why can't I let it go? Just dismiss her as another pretty girl I don't have time for?

When the bell rings, Clarissa is out of her chair and instantly walking to the door. I rush to catch up to her, not giving the guys time to start talking to me.

"Hey," I say.

She looks startled. "What?"

I shrug. It's completely stupid but I can't help myself. "You want to hang out tonight?"

CHAPTER NINE

Clarissa

DID I hear that correctly or am I going crazy? We are standing in a busy hallway so his words could have gotten muddled by all the surrounding noise before they got to me. It sure sounded like he wanted to hang out. Today.

"Um, I have work," I say.

He shrugs. "I have soccer practice until five thirty. When are you off work?"

Is this really happening? "Six thirty."

"I'll pick you up at seven."

Wow. I think it is happening.

I nod dumbly. "Okay, well, do you know where I live?"

"Unfortunately, I'm not a stalker, so no." He grins and hands me his phone. "What's your number?"

I type in my number and call it so that I'll get his number, too. My fingers are shaky as I hand his phone back. This is unexpected, but when it comes to finding out who ruined my greenhouse, it's actually a great thing. It helps that Gavin is crazy hot, and also taller than me too. Even if I wasn't on a mission to solve the mystery of my greenhouse, how could I say no to spending the evening with him?

He flashes me a smile that makes my knees go weak as he puts his phone back in his pocket. I'm trying to play it cool but I no doubt look like a grinning fool right about now. Who cares? Gavin Voss just asked me out.

Or did he?

Is it a date or just a friend thing? I'm not about to sound like an idiot and ask. I'll just play it by ear, and maybe if I'm lucky, he'll lead me right to the person on his soccer team who needs to pay up for my greenhouse.

I realize he's still walking with me as we round the corner into the math hallway. I hate how much I enjoy having someone to walk next to me. "Don't you need to get to class?" I ask.

He shrugs. "I like taking the long way."

When I get to my next class, he bumps into me with his shoulder. "Have a good day."

"Thanks," I say, looking up at him and wondering how I got so lucky. "You too."

When Shawn asked me out it was because we had mutual friends who kept saying we'd make a good couple. Once I got that thought in my head, I'd gone heavy on the flirting in the hopes that he would feel the same way. Eventually, it worked. I was happy being with him, but it's always more romantic if a guy likes you first. For the first time in my life, it's starting to feel like that's what's happening.

I've had guys approach me over the years, mostly back in junior high when I wasn't so tall yet, but none of them were ever that great. They were mostly guys who annoyed me. Shawn was my first real boyfriend, and I never thought I'd attract the attention of someone like Gavin. But it kind of feels like I just did.

I think about texting Livi all during second and third period, but then I decide that news this juicy needs to be told in person. It sucks that we don't have lunch together this year because that's the only time we have to unwind during the day. Instead, I sit with Erin, who is Livi's cousin. She's a sophomore with the same blonde hair as Livi, but she keeps hers cut short in a bob. She's also crazy smart and participates in every nerd club they have at school. But she's a good friend who never spreads gossip, so although I wish Livi were here with us, at least I have someone to hang out with during lunch.

"Someone keeps staring at her phone," Erin says, giving me a curious look as she takes a bite of her sandwich. "Anything good on Snapchat?"

I shake my head. "I'm just bored." The truth is that I can't stop thinking about how I now have Gavin Voss' phone number saved and he has mine. I kind of wish Shawn could see me now, hanging out with a guy who is better than him.

Just like how Shawn's new girlfriend Mindy is better than me.

I shove the thought away and turn my attention to the pizza I got for lunch.

My phone lights up.

Gavin: Hi there

. . .

I look up. I don't know where Gavin sits, or if he's even in this lunch period, but it feels like I'm being watched. Slowly, my eyes drift over the tables until I find one with a bunch of jocks scarfing down tons of food. Gavin is staring right at me. He's flocked on both sides by his friends, but none of them are paying attention to him. He grins and types something on this phone.

Gavin: You should come sit with me

I swallow the bite of food in my mouth and glance over at Erin, who is busy trying to open her can of soda without messing up her manicure.

Me: I don't want to leave my friend

Gavin: Bring her

I glance back at him and he's talking with TJ, who's sitting next to him. He looks back over at me a moment later. He lifts an eyebrow and nods his head in a motion that's telling me to join him.

I text him back.

. . .

Me: Big table of jocks isn't my idea of a good lunch break

I watch him read my text from across the room. He laughs and then smacks one of his friends as they steal some fries off his lunch tray.

Gavin: Understandable.

Me: Are we still on for tonight?

Gavin: of course

I bite down on my lip to keep from smiling. What is this? What's happening? I mean, to an outsider it would seem that the gorgeous Gavin Voss is flirting with me. But I'm scared to let myself bask in that feeling until I know it's true.

Somehow, I manage to get through the rest of lunch without saying anything about him to Erin. It's not that I don't want her to know, but Livi is my best friend and I should tell her first. Which is exactly what I do the very second the final bell rings.

I rush out of my last class and head toward the hallway where Livi's locker is. I meet her there right when she does and I grab her arm as she's messing with her locker combination.

"I have news."

"Did they catch the greenhouse guys?" She shoves her textbook into her locker and then slams the door closed.

"No, but this is better. Well...it's good. It's not better. We still need to find those guys, but this might actually help me do it."

"Okay, I'm intrigued," she says, looping her arm through mine as we make our way toward the bus lot.

"We have to be alone first," I say. "Too many people could overhear right now."

"Oh crap, now I have to know!"

I grin. "I've been dying to tell you all freaking day."

As soon as we're outside, I pull her to the edge of the bus pickup line. I glance around, and when no one is within earshot, I say, "I'm pretty sure Gavin Voss just asked me on, like, a date."

Livi's eyes go wide. "The soccer player? Tall guy?"

I nod eagerly. "Holy shit," she breathes. "That's amazing! I mean, *duh*. I know you're beautiful and smart and perfect for any guy, but I'm just glad someone like him was smart enough to see it, too."

"I love you and your loyalty," I say with a laugh. "I am not that great. I don't know why he did, but he asked if I want to hang out tonight and he's going to pick me up at my house and everything."

"Well, a date on a Wednesday is kind of awesome. It means he likes you so much he can't wait until the weekend."

My good mood falters. "Or it means he doesn't like me that much and would rather save the weekend for hotter girls he likes more."

She rolls her eyes. "No. If he didn't like you, he wouldn't have asked you out. I bet he also wants to hang this weekend. Oh my God, I'm so excited for you!"

"Don't say anything, okay?" I can feel my phone in my back pocket, but suddenly I want to check it, just to confirm that his texts earlier were real and not all in my imagination. "I don't want people to think I'm making more out of it than it is."

"Girl, I got you." Livi wiggles her eyebrows. "You need to change your mindset. Gavin Voss is lucky to be seen with you. He should be begging to have your attention."

I laugh. "Okay, sure, I can play pretend too."

The teacher on duty yells out that everyone needs to hurry and get on the bus. Freaking school is always on a schedule, and I hardly ever see my best friend.

"I'll tell you what happens," I say as we rush to our buses.

"Every single detail!" Livi calls back to me.

I jog up the bus stairs and swing into an empty seat near the back. The whole ride home I can't stop thinking about Gavin and our "hang out" session tonight. What will he want to do? Is it a date? Or will we watch TV at my house? What should I wear?

As much as I hope it *is* a date, and that Gavin actually likes me, I also don't mind if it's just a friend thing. Because for the first time since Shawn dumped me, I'm feeling hopeful about the idea of dating again. All those talks about broken hearts needing time are totally right. I feel healed now. Like I can fully move on and get excited about a guy again.

On top of all of this, Fate has handed me something extra special. A member of the soccer team. If I can just flirt enough to win him over, maybe he'll tell me exactly what I want to know.

CHAPTER TEN

GAVIN

EVEN AFTER A LONG HOT SHOWER, my legs are killing me. Coach had us do thirty minutes of burpees and then an hour and a half of sprints. Soccer players can run, but even we hate an hour and a half of sprints.

I could really use a nap right now, but what I want more than that is to spend some time with Clarissa. I pull into her driveway and rub my sore thighs for a second before getting out.

I'm here, I text her, because she'd asked me to let her know the second I arrive.

When I get up to the door and ring the doorbell, I'm a little surprised at the nervous feeling in my stomach. It's stupid because I've dated plenty of girls. I've done this plenty of times. Parents always love me.

The door swings open and an older man stands there, looking at me like he's not too happy with what he sees.

"Hello," I say, standing tall. "I'm here to pick up Clarissa."

He squints at me. "What's your name?"

"Gavin," I say. "Gavin Voss, sir."

"I don't know you, right?"

"That's right."

He nods. "Okay, well nice to meet you."

He doesn't hold out his hand to shake mine. He also doesn't look me in the eyes. I wonder if he's trying to intimidate me. Clarissa appears behind him. "Grandpa, I've got it. Thanks."

She steps in front of him and takes his shoulders, turning him around. "Thank you. I'll be home in a little bit."

"That's Gavin Voss," her grandpa says. "I think he likes you. He certainly sounds nervous."

She steps outside and closes the door behind her. "Sorry about that," she says sheepishly. "My grandpa is mostly blind. I told you to text me so I could be at the door first!"

"I did text you," I say, offering my arm to her.

"You didn't text me fast enough! We could have avoided that awkwardness."

"I don't mind it." I keep my elbow out and she finally looks down, noticing it for the first time.

She chews on her bottom lip as her fingers reach out and tentatively wrap around my elbow. I tug my arm closer to my side and she comes with it.

"Are you hungry?" I ask.

"Are you?" she says.

"I'm always hungry. I thought we could go down to the boardwalk. There's a diner there that's amazing."

"The pie place?" she asks. I'm keenly aware of her strawberry smelling hair and the gloss on her lips that might taste like the same thing.

"Yeah, it's called The Apple Pie. It's only been there a few months but the food is amazing."

"That sounds fun. I've heard a lot of people talk about it."

We get to my truck, and I open the door for her. Only now do I realize what she's wearing. I'd been so focused on her face that I hadn't looked down.

She's wearing tight jeans that are cuffed on the bottom, and black ballerina shoes. I know from experience in homeroom that her ass probably looks amazing in them, but I'm not about to turn her around and find out. At least not on our first date. Her shirt has long sleeves and it falls off her shoulder on one side. The smooth skin there drives me crazy.

"Thank you," she says, climbing into my truck. I wink at her as I close the door behind her.

I am really good at this dating thing, and I'm going to prove that to her tonight.

At the boardwalk, I find a parking spot next to the Flying Mermaid, which is a surf shop that supplies pretty much all of the clothes I wear all summer.

"I haven't been to the beach in a while," Clarissa says as we make our way toward the restaurant. The boardwalk stretches on for a few miles along the Texas coast. There are tons of stores and restaurants along the way, and beyond the wooden railing is the beach for as far as you can see. Since it's the end of August, there's still enough summertime left for the surfers to be out enjoying the waves.

"I come here as much as I can," I say. I want to reach for her hand, but I know it's too soon for that. "Lately all I do is work and play soccer, so there's not much time for it."

"The only thing stopping me is that I don't have a car," she says. The breeze blows her hair around and she runs her fingers through it to straighten it out. "I'm one of the only juniors at the school who has no wheels."

"That's no fun," I say, holding open the door to The Apple Pie for her. "Took me three years of working to save up for mine. I actually started mowing lawns when I was fourteen just for the sole purpose of buying my truck."

"Wow, way to plan ahead. I'm saving my money for college, but the daycare does not pay very much. And it's only three hours a day, a few times a week." She makes this face and it's so cute I want to kiss it off her.

But I have to keep my hands to myself, at least for now. *Be a gentleman, Gavin.*

"If you ever need a ride and I'm free, I'd be happy to drive you wherever you want to go."

She stares into her soda. "Thanks."

"I'm serious," I say. "That wasn't some empty offer."

"Do you make empty offers often?" she asks in this teasing way.

I shrug. "Sometimes, yeah. But only to the jackasses I call friends."

"Well, at least you're honest," she says with a playful grin.

We get our food and eat it on the restaurant's balcony that overlooks the beach. I am terrified that the conversation will lag, so I try to keep talking.

"So what's your schedule like this year?"

Inwardly, I cringe. That's about the lamest question you can ask a girl on a first date.

"Let's see," she says, counting off on her fingers. "Boring, boring, boring, boring, and boring. The only class I really like is my sixth period Sign Language class."

"I took French, but I wish I'd taken Sign Language," I say. "Then I could have secret conversations in class."

"We already can," she says with a coy smile. "It's called text messaging. It lets you talk without verbally saying anything. You should look it up."

"I see how it is," I say, fixing her with a stare. "You go out with a guy, looking cute as hell, and then you rag on him for not being a genius."

She stops laughing and her expression turns serious. "So, *is* this a date?"

"Yes," I say, wondering if I haven't made that part clear.

"Like a real date?" she asks, her voice getting a little bit higher.

I nod and bite on a French fry. "I mean, I want it to be a real date. I fully intend on buying your dinner and refusing you if you try to pay for part of it."

Her cheeks turn a glorious shade of pink. "Okay. I was just wondering."

"Do you often go out with guys and it's not a date?" I ask.

She shakes her head. "I mean, all signs pointed to this being a date, but I wasn't sure. So I just wanted to ask and get it out in the open." She puts her hands on her face. "Am I ruining this?"

"No," I say, reaching out and pulling her hand down. I let my fingers slide down her arm, down her palm, and across her fingertips. "I'm having a really good time making you nervous." I grin and she glares at me, her lips pressing together.

"Not very gentlemanly of you, Gavin."

"I'll behave," I say. We talk for a while about every random topic we can think of. School, mostly, and a little about how her friend Livi also doesn't have a car so they rarely get to hang out after school. When our food is done, I stand up and hold out my hand.

"Want to walk on the beach? That's a fun date thing to do."

"Yeah, okay," she says, standing. I hold out my hand closer to hers and she eyes it before sliding her palm into mine. "First time for everything," she says softly as we walk away.

I stop right in the middle of the sand. "Wait, what?" I hold up our clasped hands. "Is this your first time holding hands on the beach?"

She nods meekly. "Kind of?"

My brows pull together. "What kind of guys have you been dating?"

She shrugs. "First of all, not very many. And secondly, guys who don't like being seen with me."

She looks away and I start walking toward the water, keeping her hand grasped in mine. "Now why wouldn't a guy want to be seen with you? You are totally beautiful and very much rocking those jeans, by the way."

When she glances up at me, there's a spark in her eyes I haven't seen before. Something tells me she doesn't get complimented much. I make it my personal mission right here and now to tell her how unbelievably cute she I at all times.

"Let's not talk about ... that stuff," she says after a moment. "It's just—awkward."

I gaze at her, trying to figure out what insecurity she's hiding behind those brown eyes. But I come up empty, because the girl is adorable in every way.

On the sand, the water rushes over our feet and then sweeps back out to sea. "Tell me something about you," I say.

"Not much more to tell," she says quickly. "I go to school, and I work at the daycare. I have exactly zero hidden talents."

"Hidden talents are overrated," I say. "Do you like working at the daycare?"

She nods. "The kids are so sweet. I'm pretty sure I want to be a kindergarten teacher, but my mom says those kinds of jobs are more stressful than they seem."

"You'll never know unless you try it," I say.

"What about you?" she asks, nudging me with her elbow. "Some kind of rocket scientist? Brain surgeon?"

"Do I look like a rocket scientist?" I ask.

She laughs. "No, but you're in all those AP classes."

"*So* jealous of my mad school skills," I tease her. "I wish I could take the credit for it, but school stuff just comes easily to me."

She pokes me in the stomach with her free hand. "I'm not jealous of a nerd."

"I'm not a nerd," I say, pretending to look offended. "I'm a star soccer player."

She rolls her eyes. "You soccer guys are on my shit list right now."

"Why's that?" If I had taken even two seconds to think before I speak, I would have remembered why. But of course, I didn't, because I'm caught up in the smell of Clarissa's shampoo, the quirk of her lips every time I tease her. I'm also kind of checking out her cleavage in a way that's turning me on but making me feel like a dick about it. It's not my fault that she's so captivating that I can't think clearly.

Her expression darkens. "Because two of your teammates ruined my greenhouse."

"But it's going to get rebuilt, though, right?"

She sighs. "I have no idea. Probably not."

"Why?"

She turns away from me, letting her gaze drift over the ocean. "I'd rather not talk about it."

She's told me she loves kids and she liked the greenhouse, but I can't see why she'd be so damn upset about it. But she clearly doesn't want me to push the topic, so I don't.

"I'm sorry someone ruined it," I say, feeling a tightness in my chest. This lie is so deeply buried in my heart now that even *I'm* starting to think I didn't actually do it.

She slows down, digging her toes in the sand. Her hand falls away from mine and suddenly I hate that she seems so far away. I want to be touching her, getting to know her. She folds her arms over her chest, not caring when the wind whips her hair into her eyes.

"Do you know who did it?" she asks softly.

"What do you mean?" I say.

Her head tilts up at me, her eyes filled with sadness. "You're all a team. Surely the other guys talk with each other. Do you know and you're just supposed to keep it a secret?"

Guilt claws at my insides. This girl is smart. Part of me wonders if she's only here tonight as a way to get information out of me. That thought alone rips into my ego and makes my heart ache. I'm really starting to like her. She's gorgeous, she's funny, and sweet. She's the kind of girl who cares so damn much about some dumb greenhouse just because she works there.

That's the kind of girl who makes a great girlfriend. One

who cares about things besides herself. She's the kind of girl I need in my life. She could be the light when I'm surrounded by all the darkness that makes me want to drink.

I swallow the lump in my throat. "I don't know who did it," I say, reaching for her hand again. "I'm sorry."

CHAPTER ELEVEN

Clarissa

WE SIT on a bench at the end of the boardwalk. It's far away from the few remaining people out here, and tucked under the glow of the last street lamp, it feels romantic. The ocean crashes to shore and then falls back, the sounds of the water and the seagulls flying above reminding me of summer. It also reminds me of being a kid and playing on this beach when I didn't have a care in the world.

Gavin's arm is across the back of the bench, and I lean back, letting my back press against the slats. As if on instinct, his arm tucks closer to me, his fingers curving around my shoulder. The touch sends a shiver down to my toes. All I'd have to do is lean a little to the left and I'd be snuggled against his chest.

I take a quick breath and gaze out at the ocean and remind myself of one thing: *First date. First date. First date.*

I keep wanting to take it further. To cuddle and hold his hand again and, well, even the thought of this sends a ball of heat into my belly, but I want to kiss him.

Gavin is nothing like that cocky jerk who had his feet on

my chair that first day of school. He's sweet and attentive. He pays attention when I talk, his blue eyes focused just on me. He's not like Shawn, who would gaze off and look at other things, only half listening to anything I had to say.

He's not like Shawn in a lot of ways.

"You seem very deep in thought," Gavin says after a moment.

I shrug. "Just enjoying the beach."

"You sure?" His eyes peer down into mine, his eyebrows raised a bit in concern. "You've gotten extra quiet."

"I'm fine," I say, smiling so he knows I mean it. "We've pretty much talked ourselves out tonight, don't you think? You might know me better than my own best friend knows me."

That's not exactly true. While I've shared many things with Gavin tonight, I haven't told him about my greenhouse and what it means to me. Part of me wants to tell him, to let him know how important it is that I find who ruined it. Maybe if he knew the truth, he'd go face-to-face with his own team mates until they told him. But I can't bring myself to say anything. It's just too close to my heart. It's too raw right now.

I only briefly mentioned that my Grandpa was mostly blind when he picked me up at my house. I didn't tell him it only just now happened and that we're struggling to learn how to live with a blind family member. I haven't told him about my grandma and her greenhouse. We've talked all night about silly things, but nothing that really matters. But this is a first date, so we're not supposed to get too deep. Maybe one day, if he still likes me after tonight, he'll get to learn all those things about me.

"Do you think we talked too much?" Gavin asks as his

fingers trace circles on my shoulder. I wish he'd move his hand down, slide it around my waist, or entwine his fingers into mine.

"No," I say playfully. "I like taking to you. I've liked this whole night."

He grins like I've just complimented him. "Me too. I'm not sure what speed to take this but—I just can't stop talking. I don't want to take time getting to know you, I want to know you immediately."

He breathes in deeply and then lets it out. "Does that make sense? Am I insane?"

Now I'm the one grinning. "No, I get it. Why haven't we ever met before now?"

"Probably because you were too busy to notice that kick ass soccer player with the great hair."

I elbow him in the ribs. "Yeah, right. You were probably too busy dating all kinds of hot girls to notice me."

"There's a massive flaw in your logic," he says. He reaches over and tucks my hair behind my ear, even though the wind from the beach will just knock it out again in a few minutes. "If I was dating hot girls, then I would have already dated you. So...flawed logic."

I snort. "Coming on strong with the compliments, eh?"

He squeezes me closer to his chest. "I've got better ones than that."

I roll my eyes and look away, suddenly feeling very embarrassed. Unfortunately, that only encourages him.

"Let's see... You are definitely the hottest girl in the school."

"Lies!" I say.

He talks over me, "You've got eyes the color of honey and

I just want to look into them all damn night. You smell like an angel. Also—yeah, that," he says, nodding at me. "That smile. It's adorable."

"Okay, okay," I say, holding up my hands. "You've proven that you can sling around some compliments. I don't need to hear anymore."

"They're all true," he says. "And trust me, I could still go on."

I fold my arms over my chest and give him a disbelieving look. "All of those compliments could have been used on any girl. Don't ruin this awesome night by busting out your Casanova moves on me. Just be yourself."

"I am being myself, Clarissa." His voice is a touch deeper as he leans over, his lips brushing against mine while he whispers, "You've been teasing me with that bare collarbone all night, so much that I'm surprised I haven't spontaneously combusted yet."

"Wait, what?"

I look down. My shirt has a loose neck that's supposed to slouch down over one shoulder. I wore it tonight because the long sleeves would keep me warm without a jacket.

"I didn't know collar bones were sexy," I say, absentmindedly touching mine. "I mean, boobs, yeah. Obviously. But a bone in your shoulder?"

"Totally, unbelievably hot," he says.

I give him a look. I know he's trying to pull out the big guns with his compliments, but I'm not buying it.

He lifts an eyebrow. "Don't believe me?"

I shake my head.

With one arm still around my shoulders, his other hand brushes my hair to one side. His eyes pour into mine as he leans closer, and then dips his head into the crook of my neck. I go completely still. I can feel his breath on my skin, hear my heart beat in my head.

Gavin's warm lips press to my collarbone in a slow, seductive kiss. I close my eyes as his fingers slide across my shoulder, his rough skin sending goosebumps down my chest. He kisses a trail from my shoulder up to my neck, keeping his movements slow, sensual in a way that makes me stop breathing.

I'm not ready for this to end, but he pulls away, making me whimper in the back of my throat.

"Told you," he whispers into my ear.

"Holy hell," I breathe. Every nerve in my body is on fire, and it's going to take me a minute to get back to normal. But deep down, I don't want to go back to normal. I want him to wrap me back up in his arms and do that again.

After gazing out at the ocean quietly for a while, Gavin reaches over and grabs my leg. In one smooth motion, he pulls my knees across his legs, and then suddenly I'm sitting in his lap.

How the hell did he do that?

I wrap an arm around his neck for stability, and keep the other one in my lap, even though I really want to run it down his chest. When I'd poked him in the stomach earlier, all I'd felt was hard, smooth muscle. I want to know if the rest of him feels that way, too.

"I think there's enough room on this bench for both of us," I say playfully.

"I like this way better." His hand slides down my thigh, sending a shiver down to my toes. His eyes widen. "I mean, if you don't like this, we don't have to—"

I shake my head. "It's fine."

He looks relieved. "You just tell me if I'm moving too fast. I don't want you to feel uncomfortable."

I know some guys say that shit, but right now with Gavin, it looks like he actually believes it. My heart warms a little more for him. And now I think I'm definitely in danger of falling for this guy. Like—hard. Head over heels, swoony-eye emoji, grinning all day, kind of falling.

"Thank you for this date," I say, still holding back on the desire to run my hand across his chest.

"It's after ten on a school night," he says with a frown. "I should probably get you back home."

I nod, knowing my mom and grandpa are asleep and probably won't even care what time I'm back. But deep down I know I need to maintain a little mystery, be a little inaccessible. If I want him to keep liking me, I can't become clingy.

And I definitely want him to keep liking me.

Before I know it, we're in my driveway, and Gavin is walking me up to the door.

"You're a real gentleman," I say, batting my eyelashes at him. "Walking me to the door and everything."

"I'm just making sure you get home safely. For all I know, a murderer could be hiding in those bushes." He points to the mostly dead bush by our front door. The summer heat wave didn't leave many of our plants alive.

I laugh. "Well, thank you for keeping the murderers away."

I know what comes next—the awkward goodbye after a first date. I had this with Shawn, too, and he ended up pulling me in for a quick hug and then jogging back to his truck.

Eventually, things got more normal for us, but the awkward first date phase is the worst.

Gavin takes my fingertips in his, our hands just barely touching as we stand here in the dark, facing each other. "I want to kiss you," he says softly.

"Why?" I ask. He lifts an eyebrow, and I realize I sounded kind of harsh. I let my shoulders fall. "I mean... why do you want to? Because it's a first date and it's like, tradition? Or—"

"Because you're amazing in every way," he says, cutting me off. He takes a step closer and releases my fingers, then cups my face in his hands. "Because ever since you knocked my feet off your chair, I've been totally stuck on you, wanting you to like me. I felt like I had to win you over, and now it feels like I might actually have a chance." His hands slide down to my shoulders. "I'm crazy about you, Clarissa. That's why." His tongue flicks across his bottom lip and he smiles at me. "But I can take my time. If you don't want to, that's fine with me."

I draw in a ragged breath. That little monologue of his has awakened something inside of me. This passionate, aching, hungry part of me that I don't think has ever been awake until now. I peer up at him, silently thanking the Universe for making him taller than I am, for letting me bask in this moment like a normal girl who isn't freakishly tall.

"It's just that first kisses are kind of a big moment."

"Is this moment big enough?" he asks softly. "I can come back on horseback, with flowers. A thousand flowers."

I chuckle and press my hands on his chest. "I don't need pomp and circumstance," I say playfully. "I just need—I don't know—honesty."

"You are *honestly* the best thing in my life right now," Gavin whispers, lowering his forehead to mine.

"So do it," I whisper back. "Kiss me."

And he does. Without hesitation, Gavin takes me into his arms and pulls me into him. Our lips press together, packed with all the anticipation of this whole night. I forget to breathe at first, all these thoughts of technique and skill making me nervous. I want him to like me and I want him to like kissing me.

But Gavin knows what he's doing. His lips move over mine in ways that send heat coursing through my body. His lips part slightly, so I part mine, and then his head tilts and he's kissing me gently, like he did to my collarbone. It drives me crazy. I bury my hands into his short hair, tugging him down closer to me.

He deepens the kiss, and my knees nearly go out when his tongue flicks across my bottom lip. But he's holding onto me tightly, his strong arms keeping me pressed against him.

When we finally break apart, I am out of breath, and my lips are tingling. Gavin's cute smile reaches his eyes. "Goodnight," he whispers.

"Goodnight," I say back. He steps backward while I slip into my house, and as I close the door, I'm only thinking one thing.

His chest does feel as amazing as I thought it would.

CHAPTER TWELVE

GAVIN

I'M COMPLETELY EXHAUSTED when I wake up the next morning, but I couldn't be happier. Coach can make us do drills for twelve hours straight, and nothing will take away the thrill of meeting Clarissa.

I lay in bed for way too long, reliving our perfect first date together. I can still feel her lips, taste her lip gloss, and remember the smell of her when I held her close to me.

This is the start of something amazing. I can feel it.

Mom's made scrambled eggs this morning, and I scarf them down quickly and then give her a hug, which seems to surprise her. But I can't help myself, I am in a fantastic mood.

At school, I take the first parking spot I find, and then I rush into the building. I should have thought ahead and asked Clarissa if I could drive her to school. She lives just a few blocks down from me, so it would be no trouble at all, and it'd mean I get to spend even more time with her.

But for now, my mission will be seeing if she'll let me eat lunch with her and her friends. It dawns on me that I haven't even told the guys that I've got a new girl yet. Oh well, they don't need to know. They'd only make crass comments like they do with every girl I date. For now, this epic new beginning with the girl of my dreams is just between us. And I like it.

Clarissa isn't in her desk when I get to homeroom. I keep my eyes on the door, waiting for her to come inside, but soon the bell rings and she's still missing.

I take out my phone to text her but the teacher clears her throat. "No phones in class."

With a groan, I slide my phone back in my pocket. The announcements come on, and I'm still glancing at the door, wondering if she's just late.

And then the teacher's office phone rings. "Mr. Voss?" she says, catching me off guard. "You're wanted in the office."

I grab my bag and notice TJ glaring at me as I walk past him. He's an idiot, though. If they'd actually caught us, they'd be calling him too. Who knows what this is about.

The office secretary tells me to head down to Principal Walsh's office. My heartbeat picks up pace because usually a visit to the principal is not a good thing.

My heart nearly stops when I enter the room and see Clarissa sitting there as well. Relief pours over me once I know she's here at school and not home sick, or worse—avoiding me. She looks surprised when she sees me, but then her lips tip into a sheepish smile. I wink at her.

"Have a seat," Principal Walsh says, pointing to the chair next to Clarissa. To her, he says, "It looks like Linda isn't in town. She's asked me to relay the information to you and you make the final call."

"Okay," Clarissa says, her voice sounding a little choked. She looks over at me.

I have no idea who Linda is, or why the two of us are called into the principal's office. It's not like making out on a girl's porch is against school rules. It has nothing to do with the school.

Principal Walsh laces his fingers together on top of his desk, and he focuses his gaze on me. "Gavin, you're a member of the junior's soccer team?"

"Yes." I'm barely able to hear myself talk over the sound of my own heart. Please, God, don't let this be what I think it is. Not here. Not in front of Clarissa.

The principal clears his throat. "I know it was you, Gavin. You destroyed the greenhouse."

Silence pierces through the room. I glance over at Clarissa, but she's staring straight ahead, unmoving, and her jaw set.

"I don't understand," I begin, trying like crazy to think up a good excuse. A reason, an explanation. She can't hear this. Not here, not now. Not this way.

"I think you do understand, Mr. Voss. We have video evidence that two soccer players wearing the hoodie that only the junior team has are the culprits in this vandalism case. After tireless inquiries, we have discovered that every other member of the team has an alibi for where they were that night. Everyone except you."

"You didn't even ask me for an alibi!" I say, suddenly feeling so left in the dark. They've been questioning my teammates this whole time and no one told me? What about TJ? He shouldn't have an alibi.

"We also received three anonymous tips that name you as the culprit. One even said you were heard bragging about giving your extra hoodie to a friend to wear that night."

My mouth falls open. Of all the truth in this, that I did the vandalism, this is covered in lies.

Clarissa still hasn't said a word. I don't even think she's moved.

"There is no point in denying it, Mr. Voss. I measured the height of the one remaining wall of that greenhouse. Six foot six inches. On the video, you can be seen standing right next to it. You are the only member of the soccer team who is nearly that height." His voice gets higher with each word he says. "Are you really going to sit here and deny something that we both know is true?"

Fear crashes into me. I am not afraid of the principal or the soccer coach. But I am afraid of one thing.

"Please don't tell my parents." My hands shake with the mere thought of what my dad would do if he knew. "Please—I—my dad, he can't find out. I'll do anything."

"Perhaps you should have thought of the consequences when you were committing the vandalism, Mr. Voss. You are still a minor, and alerting your parents is the next thing on my list."

"Please don't!" I'm begging. Crumbling in front of the girl I care about. I take a deep breath. "I'll do anything. I can pay to have it fixed. I'll do community service. Anything, please. You can't tell them. Or tell my mom if you have to, but not my dad. Please, sir."

Principal Walsh gives me a curious look.

For the first time since I got here, Clarissa speaks up. "Don't tell his parents," she says, her voice sounding resigned.

I look over gratefully at her, pleading with my eyes for her to forgive me. She looks away.

"Very well," Principal Walsh says with a heavy sigh. "I

won't tell your parents at this moment. However, you will pay for the cost of rebuilding the greenhouse."

"Yes," I say. "Of course."

He goes on, "You will help Miss Vale rebuild the greenhouse."

"I'll be happy to."

She scowls.

Principal Walsh continues, "And you are kicked off the soccer team."

The words hit me like a punch to the gut. Soccer has been my one constant since I was five years old. It's where my heart is. Where my friends are. It's the sole source of every friendship I have, both on the team and off it. I am a soccer player. That's who I am.

But the other option is impossible. I lower my head and swallow the lump in my throat. "Yes, sir."

"If you make good on your promise to fix the greenhouse, then I see no reason why your parents will need to be contacted. However, should they inquire about why you're off the team—"

"They won't," I say, trying not to snort sarcastically. "They don't care what I do in school."

He nods once. "I will let Linda Bradley know that you've agreed to fix what you've done. You're lucky that she doesn't want to press charges, son. I hope you'll learn a lesson from this."

"I have," I say, glancing at Clarissa again, but she's pretending I don't exist. "I swear I'll never do anything like that again."

"Good. You're dismissed."

Clarissa bolts out of her chair and slips out of the office before I can even catch my breath.

"Thank you," I tell the principal and then I grab my backpack and rush after her. She's already out of the main office and down the hallway, walking like she's afraid a monster is chasing her.

Is that what I am?

I can't be. I'm a good guy. I made a mistake.

I lied to her. But that won't happen again.

"Clarissa!" I call out, jogging to catch up with her. "Hey. Wait, please."

She clenches her jaw but she keeps walking, even with me by her side. I was worried she might actually run away from me.

"Please," I say, touching her shoulder.

"Don't touch me." Her words are venom, and I yank my hand away.

"Clarissa, please. Let me explain."

"There is nothing to explain," she says, stopping quickly. She meets my gaze, and her eyes are hard, angry, and nothing like they were last night. "You lied to me."

I go to say something but she holds up a hand, stopping me. "Don't talk to me. I will get you a list of supplies for my greenhouse and then we are never speaking again."

She turns and storms off, leaving me right where I belong. Alone, with my mouth open like the asshole that I am.

Thursdays are always busy at Magic Mark's Pizza. Sometimes they're even busier than the weekend, and no one knows why.

It's just a pizza phenomenon I suppose. I keep my truck running as I head inside and grab the next delivery order. Then I rush out to my truck and take it to its destination.

The night goes on, and all I do is focus on work. If I let my mind wander even a little, I feel my heart tear to shreds. I hate myself.

I want to call TJ and ask him what the hell is going on. Why I got busted, and why he supposedly has an alibi. But if I talk to him now, I'll probably explode. So for now, I focus on the pizza.

I let my boss know I'm free every day now, not just Tuesdays and Thursdays. He seems happy with this and says I can come in tomorrow and help with deliveries.

Just twenty-four hours ago, I'd thought my Friday would be spent on another romantic date with Clarissa.

How wrong I was.

Mom calls me around nine, and I answer the call between deliveries.

"Hi, son," she says. Her voice sounds tired like it does in the mornings even though she only just now got to work. "I have a favor to ask of you."

"What is it?"

"We don't have enough money for the cable bill," she says, following it with a sigh. "I keep saying we should just cancel the damn thing but your dad likes the sports channels."

"How much do you need?" I ask.

"One sixty. I don't know if you have any money but..."

"I've got it," I say. I look over at my empty passenger seat, remembering when Clarissa sat there, making my whole world amazing. "I'll leave the cash on the kitchen table for you when I get off work."

"You're a sweetheart," Mom says. If only she knew the truth of what her son has become. A liar. A vandal. An asshole. "I'll pay you back as soon as I can."

"Don't worry about it, Mom. I live there, too. I can help pay the bills."

"You're such a wonderful son," Mom says. I can hear the smile in her voice and it fills me with shame. "If we could not tell your dad about this...I just don't want him to know we were short on cash again this month. You know how he is."

"I know," I say softly. "I've got your back, Mom."

"Thanks, Gavin."

When the call is over, I drop my forehead to my steering wheel. Maybe it's a good thing I can't play soccer right now. I need these extra shifts at work if I'm going to pay for a greenhouse and help my mom with the bills, on top of my own bills like gas, car insurance, and my cell phone.

But still, it's hard to see the good in anything right now.

CHAPTER THIRTEEN

Clarissa

IT'S after seven by the time Livi finally gets here. I've been pacing by the living room window, watching for her mom's Prius to pull into the driveway and drop her off. Getting through today was a complete nightmare, and as soon as I saw her after school, I nearly burst into tears. But I couldn't tell her anything there, not with all the people around.

Instead, I begged her to spend the night tonight. Thank God, it's Friday and I won't have to go back to homeroom for another two days. Even then, I'm considering heading to the courthouse and legally changing my last name so they'll put me in a different homeroom class. A little dramatic, yes, but then I'll never have to see Gavin again.

I rush to the front door and pull it open just as Livi walks up. I wave at her mom as she backs out of the driveway.

"Have you eaten?" Livi asks, holding up a pizza box. "I haven't, so I got something on the way."

The smell of Magic Mark's pepperoni pizza makes my mouth water, which is a nice feeling because I haven't eaten all day. After being completely blindsided in the office first thing in the morning, my appetite disappeared. But now it's back, and I take the pizza box from my best friend.

"I'm starving. Let's sneak this to my room."

"I heard that," Mom says, appearing in the foyer.

Shit. She puts one hand on her hip and gives me a Mom Look, then she turns to Livi. "Hi, Livi. How are you?"

"I'm doing okay. I wish summer break wasn't so short."

Mom laughs. "Enjoy it while you can. Once you're out of school, it's work every day."

All this small talk is killing me. I've already felt like a bundle of anxiety and anger since this morning, and I'm tired of holding onto it. I need my best friend.

"Let's eat fast. I have way too many things to tell you," I say.

Mom sighs. "Oh, what the hell. You can eat that in your room, but if you spill even a crumb of it, I'll be pissed. And you'll attract roaches, which should be punishment enough."

Mom has a very strict no eating in the rooms policy. I blink. "Really?"

She nods. "Sure. You're almost an adult so I'm going to go crazy and trust you to keep your room clean. Don't spill anything."

"We won't," Livi says. "Thank you, Ms. Vale."

We grab some drinks and napkins and then head into my room. As soon as the door closes behind me, Livi's eyes widen. "Tell me *everything*."

Everything is a lot. I'm still trying to process everything. Livi has only been caught up just a small bit on the date I had on Wednesday because I'd called her right after and gushed to her. Then we just haven't had time to catch up lately.

I sit on the floor so as not to get pizza grease on my bed by accident, and open the pizza box between us. "Gavin is the one who ruined my greenhouse."

Just saying the words feels wrong. Impossible. Like I'm living in some parallel version of my life where that amazing date with Gavin never actually happened.

But I was there, and I saw his face, saw the fear beneath his eyes when he thought his parents would find out. I don't know why I stood up for him like I did—he certainly doesn't deserve it. But he just seemed so unbelievably desperate in the moment, that I had to ask the principal not to tell his parents.

Livi's jaw falls open. "You're kidding, right?"

I shake my head.

"But...Gavin is the guy you went on a date with?"

I nod.

"And.... he's also the guy who ruined your greenhouse?"

Another nod.

Her brows pull together. She takes a hair tie off her wrist and pulls back her golden curls, tightening them into a bun on the top of her head. She hardly ever does that unless she's at home because she likes to keep her hair looking gorgeous in public. But this isn't public, and this is some serious shit we're about to talk about. The hair thing seems necessary.

"I don't understand," she says, staring at the untouched pizza between us. "I mean, it happened before you met him, right? So he didn't know it was yours."

"None of that matters, Livi. He did it. *That's* the only thing that matters. He did it, and he lied."

"What do you mean he lied?"

I sigh heavily. In order to fully sulk through this pain, I need to tell her all of the details. So I do. I start with that day in homeroom, and the flirty texts at lunch, and then the date. I tell her about how I opened myself up to him, let him know all kinds of things about me.

Her lips dip into a frown as I tell her the worst part. "He looked me dead in the eyes and said he didn't know who did it."

I laugh deliriously. "The funny part? I actually believed him. I *kissed* him. I believed him and I let myself like him, and I kissed him and all along, he was just pulling one over on me. He knew the whole time and he just lied."

"Maybe he was falsely accused," she says.

I shake my head. "The principal had all this evidence. Apparently, every other guy on the team has an alibi for that time and he doesn't. He admitted it, Livi. He's going to pay for the damage and he has to help me rebuild it."

She crinkles her nose. "Do you think you can handle being with him to rebuild it?"

I shrug. "I haven't gotten that far, yet."

She puts a hand on my shoulder. "I'm so sorry, Rissa."

I grab a slice of pizza and take a bite just so I don't have to talk for a minute. I'm still hungry, but thinking about seeing Gavin again makes my stomach hurt. How can someone so cute be such an asshole?

"We could find something he loves and vandalize it," Livi says with an evil, but playful grin.

"His truck," I mutter, remembering how he went on and on about how much he loves it. He keeps it clean and smelling like Armor-all. I sigh. "Not really, Liv. Stop that scheming face. We are better than this."

She pouts. "We should still make him pay. And not just monetarily."

I nod. "I've been thinking about it. I'm supposed to make a list of all the materials he has to replace, and now I'm thinking of making him help me rebuild an even better greenhouse."

Livi's eyes narrow. "I like where this is going."

"One with better insulation, and lighting..." I take a notebook off my desk and start jotting down ideas. "All of the things we thought about adding the first time but we didn't. I was afraid the project would be too hard, but with someone else helping me who isn't as old as Grandpa...we could make it better."

"And more expensive," Livi says.

"I just don't know if I can handle it." I drop the notebook on the floor. My chest clenches up tightly like it did that whole first week after Shawn dumped me. Nothing hurts more than feeling like a huge fool. A joke. Someone who was lied to and manipulated. I can't believe I kissed him. I got all swoony eyed and giddy and stupid over him.

"God, I hate him!" I say through clenched teeth. "I hate him so much!"

"Listen, Rissa. Screw that guy. Like, seriously. You're better than him. Make him rebuild your greenhouse and then never talk to him again. This is *his* issue, not yours."

"That's just it. He should build the greenhouse to make up for what he did, but I don't even know if I want a new greenhouse anymore. I can't trust him to build it without my guidance, but I don't want to be around him."

"Yeah, I understand that," she says, her voice solemn. "Can you maybe hire a contractor to help you?"

"It's too expensive," I say, shaking my head. "Even Gavin probably can't afford that much, and contractors won't let me help them. And I *have* to help build it, or otherwise there's just no point. The whole reason I'm doing this is for my grandmother's memory."

There's a knock on my door and we both jump. I've been so caught up in my own misery that I completely forgot where I was for a minute.

"Come in," I call out.

Mom opens my door and pokes her head in, a big smile on her face. "Hey, girls!" she says cheerfully. I'm not an idiot, though. I know she's checking to make sure we haven't flung pizza all over the walls like some kind of barbarians.

"I just wanted to check in and have some girl talk," she says, stepping into my room. She tucks her brown hair behind her ears and grins at me. "How was your date?"

I'm speechless. Mom only knows that I went out with a guy. She doesn't know the end result, and I'm not about to tell her.

Luckily, Livi speaks up before too much time has passed. "Not that great," she says. "That's why we're having pizza and talking right now. Taking our mind off idiot boys."

"Aww, that's too bad." Mom reaches down and squeezes my shoulder. "You really seemed to liked hm."

"What? No, I didn't." Finally, my voice is back. And it's good at lying, it seems.

Mom's lips slide to the side of her mouth. "Well... it certainly appeared like you liked him. You were bouncing around the house the next day, all happy and giggly."

I groan. She's probably right, but I don't want to think about that. "Well, that's changed. I don't really like him. Not at all."

"Okay, okay," Mom says, bringing her fingers to her lips to turn an invisible key. "I'll shut up about it."

She leaves and closes the door behind her. I turn to Livi.

"That's it. I'm cancelling the greenhouse."

"Are you sure?"

I press my hand to my forehead, where I'm starting to get a headache. "There's just no way I can be around Gavin anymore. I hate him. He ruined my greenhouse and he ruined my heart."

There's another knock on my door. "Yes, Mom?" I call out, sounding a little more annoyed than I want to. It's not her fault I'm pissed off. But it's Grandpa who opens the door.

"I always know which room is yours," he says with a gentle smile. His eyes focus off to the side, and not at me. "Your room smells like strawberries. And...currently like pizza too, but that's unusual."

I smile. Strawberries are kind of my signature scent. I have strawberry shampoo, body wash, and strawberry air freshener in my room.

"What's up, Grandpa?" I ask. "Livi is here with me."

"I brought you something." He walks slowly into the room and then reaches into the brown paper bag he's holding. He takes out a brown bulb that kind of looks like a dirty onion.

"Is that a flower bulb?" I ask, because there's no reason he'd bring me a dirty onion.

He nods, holding it out in my general direction. I get up and take it from him. "It's a tulip bulb. Got it from Macgregor's nursery. I called them up and they delivered it to me since I can't drive anymore. You wanna know why they went through all that trouble?"

"Small town charm?" I guess.

He chuckles. "Your grandma used to visit there every week. Probably their best customer." He points at the bag. "Tulips were her favorite. I was thinking you could make this be the first thing you plant for the children at the daycare."

The lump in my throat grows to nearly the size of this tulip bulb. Grandpa still thinks our greenhouse is standing and ready for plants.

I nod slowly. "I will," I say, tucking the bulb safely back into the bag. "I promise."

CHAPTER FOURTEEN

GAVIN

AFTER SCHOOL ON FRIDAY, I head home and change clothes for work. It feels weird not going to soccer practice, but it's even weirder that none of the guys on the team even talked to me today. It's like I'm being shunned, which makes sense, I guess. I'm not on the team anymore.

Before I go to work, I text TJ.

Me: What the hell

TJ: come again?

Me: Somehow you had an alibi and I didn't?

TJ: Shit luck, dude.

Me: Are you serious?

My phone rings after that. Before I can say a word, TJ says, "You're gonna keep your mouth shut, okay?"

"Is that a threat?"

"I'm just telling you to play it smart. You should have thought of an alibi, man. They were coming around asking everyone. It's your fault, bro. I mean, it sucks, but you know you can't say anything now."

"How could I have come up with an alibi when I didn't know they were questioning everyone?" I say, my teeth gritting together.

"No one told you?" He sounds confused, but he's probably lying.

"No, TJ. No one told me. I found out when I was called to the principal's office and kicked off the team. He said every other player had an alibi, but I seem to recall you being with me that night, so how is that possible?"

"I was at my grandma's," he says. "Yep. I brought her Chinese food and did some chores around her house. She remembers."

TJ's grandma has dementia and half the time she doesn't even know who you are when you visit her.

"You're a piece of shit."

"I'm smart," he counters. "Sorry you're off the team, man, but you should have figured this out yourself. Had someone lie for you or something."

He just doesn't seem very sorry. I think of the principal saying they had three anonymous messages that all claimed I was the one who did it. I wonder if they were all written by the same person?

"Enjoy getting off scot free for something you talked me into doing, you dick."

He snorts. "See you around." And then he hangs up.

I'm so furious I almost throw my phone through the wall. Luckily, part of my brain still functions enough over all of this anger to know that phones are expensive and I can't afford a replacement.

Dad is on the phone with Mom, from the sounds of it. Yelling about money again. Funny how I can just drown out these yelling matches most of the time.

"We'll just stop wasting money," Dad says into the phone. "No more dumb shit like organic vegetables. Just live more frugally and we'll be fine."

I don't know what Mom says on the other end, but I definitely know what she's thinking. If he didn't waste so much money on beer we could buy all the organic food we wanted.

I grab my keys, head to work, and put on a smiling face. Friendly pizza delivery guys get the best tips.

On Monday, I'm actually nervous as I get to school. I've sent Clarissa one text a day since Friday, and all have gone ignored. I wanted to call her, text her more. Hell, I wanted to show up at her house and beg for forgiveness, but I'm not an idiot. I need to let her know I still care and want to make amends, but I need to do it in a way that won't drive her further away.

Now's my chance to see her again.

I walk into the school alone. All of my closest friends are on the team and they've all somehow magically disappeared from the place we usually hang out at each morning. Whatever. Assholes.

I head straight for homeroom, and I slink down in my chair. TJ and Beau come in a few minutes later.

"Sup," Beau says as he sits down. TJ ignores me.

"Just making do, I guess," I say to Beau, even though I'm not sure his question wanted an answer.

"Sorry, man," he says, giving me this pitying look. But beneath his eyes is exactly the kind of emotion I'd have if I were in his position. You can't exactly feel sorry for someone who got in trouble for doing something wrong.

That's not the whole truth, I want to yell. TJ was there too. It was his idea.

But I did it too. I participated. Hell, I had a blast destroying that greenhouse. Admitting that makes me feel the worst kind of shame. Had I known that greenhouse was being used, and that it belonged to the daycare instead of the school, and that it was *hers*, I wouldn't have touched it.

I wish I could make Clarissa believe me.

She slips into the classroom just seconds before the bell rings, which is a first for the girl who is normally here early and ready to take notes.

She doesn't make eye contact with me as she walks down the aisle and toward her desk. Just before she sits down, she slaps a paper on my desk.

"Morning," I say, but as I expect, I don't get a reply.

She sits down, leaving a wake of strawberry goodness behind her. I breathe it in slowly, remembering how it felt to be next to her at the beach. To have her in my lap. To have her lips next to mine.

I look down at the paper.

Greenhouse Supplies is written on top, followed by a list of supplies and quantities. At the bottom she's written, Estimated total: $450

Damn.

I have the money, which is good, but that's nearly all of my savings. I lean forward and say, "I'll get right on this."

She doesn't reply. Doesn't shake her head or even acknowledge that she heard me.

Clarissa Vale is back to being that cold girl she was on the first day of school.

Coach calls my name as I'm walking to my truck at the end of the day. I stop and turn around, almost wondering if I was hearing things. Coach has no reason to talk to me now. He's standing there at the end of the gym, hands on his hips. He motions for me.

I walk over there, totally not in the mood to be reamed by yet another person. My friends have shut me out, Clarissa has shut me out, and my parents are in some battle with each other that I want no part of.

"Yes, Coach?" I say, wondering what you're supposed to call a coach who isn't your coach anymore.

"I'm disappointed, Voss."

His lips press together into a thin line as he looks me over, disbelief and regret all over his face. I know he's probably thinking that I'm the only straight A student on the team. That I'm the only good one. Well, not anymore.

"Me too, sir." I sigh. "I don't even know what got into me. I don't know why. It was reckless and stupid."

"I know you weren't alone." He looks me in the eyes, giving me that same look he gives us right before we start a game against our rival team. "If you tell us who helped you, I can talk to the principal. I can try to get you reinstated."

"And kick the other guy off the team?" I say with a snort. "No thanks. I can't be a snitch."

"So it *was* another member of the team?" Coach says. I cringe. I've already said too much. "Someone's alibi was faked. Good to know that I have two liars on my team"

"Coach...it's shitty, I know. And I know it doesn't even matter anymore, but I was the one trying to stop it at first. The other guy deserves the worst punishment. Or at least equal," I say with a grimace. "But trust me. I've learned my lesson."

"Tell me who it is," he says. "I'll work with you. Try to get you back on the team."

I shake my head. TJ would kill me. He's not even a good friend, so I have no idea why I've got his back. Or maybe I do know. It's because we're a team. If I betray one of them, I betray all of them. And right now, they're all I've got.

Even though I'm pretty sure I've lost them, too.

"Sorry, Coach. I can't ruin my life more than I already have."

I leave and he doesn't stop me. I get in my truck and head straight home, grab my cash out from under my carpet, and then go to the nearest Home Depot. I buy everything on Clarissa's list and get one of the workers to help me load it up in my truck.

While my old team is still having soccer practice, I drive my truck to the place where the greenhouse used to be. I back in, parking on the grass, and then one by one, I take out all of the green paneling, wooden beams, latches, screws, and nails. I take out the door hinges and the clay pots and I set it all down neatly.

Then, although I'm sweating my ass off, I load up all of

the wreckage of what used to be the greenhouse. I see now, in the bright light of day, that these are new panels, too. Some even have the price stickers still on them. The wood is clean, the nails shiny, not rusted. This wasn't some old shack like I thought it was when I was here in the middle of the night.

Clarissa put time into making this, and I ruined it.

I haul the broken parts to the dump on my way to work. And even though I know she won't reply back, I take a photo of the materials and send it to her.

Me: I got everything on the list.

CHAPTER FIFTEEN

Clarissa

GAVIN TEXTS ME AGAIN. I know it's him before I look at my phone, because the only person who talks to me most of the time is Livi, and she uses Snapchat instead of texts.

Gavin has texted me every day, but only once per day. It's kind of weird how he's so persistent. If he thinks he'll get forgiveness, he's dead wrong.

I pick up my phone. The last few days have been a one sided conversation.

Gavin: Clarissa, I'm so sorry. I shouldn't have lied.

Gavin: I know I can't explain in a way that will make it up to you, but please talk to me.

Gavin: If I had any idea that was your greenhouse, I wouldn't have touched it. Will you talk to me?

And now, one more text today. There are no words, just a picture of a pile of greenhouse supplies on the ground. From first glance, it looks like he did buy everything I told him to. Good. I hope it was expensive.

I gnaw on the inside of my lip. Although I do plan to avoid him for the rest of my life, this is something that needs to be done. I text him back.

Me: When can we get started?

At first, I'd written *you*, as in when can *you* get started. Then I realized I have to be there. I have to supervise and help and lead the entire project if I want it to turn out right. This is the part I don't think I can handle—being around him for hours, days on end, rebuilding something my grandfather had helped me build the first time.

When my grandpa had given me that tulip bulb, Livi had suggested that I treat Gavin as if he were an anonymous contractor who had been hired to help me. If I spend the whole time pretending he's just a stranger, then maybe I can get through it.

I had fully planned on cancelling the entire thing and just lying to my grandpa forever until he brought me that tulip. I can't do that to him. I can't do it to my grandma's memory. This greenhouse needs to rise again.

So I send the stupid text and I tell myself Gavin is just a contractor, just hired help, a total stranger. To make myself believe the lie even more, I delete our chain of texts and then rename him in my contacts list. Now, instead of Gavin, he is Contractor.

It doesn't make me feel much better seeing his name like that.

Contractor: Soon, I promise.

Me: You can't give me a date?

Contractor: I'm scheduled to work several days in a row, but as soon as I'm off, I'll be there.

Me: Okay.

Contractor: Could we meet? Have coffee? Talk?

I ignore it. A contractor worth his salt would only care about the job, not taking his clients out to coffee. And from now on, that's all Gavin is to me.

I throw the phone back on my bed and I go back to reading a book I'd checked out from the library this morning. It's a teen fantasy novel with dragons and princesses and a handsome vigilante guy with a sword and a penchant for danger. There's magic and beautiful landscapes and castles. I'd hoped I could slip into this fantasy world and forget all about the real world at home. It works for a just a little bit, and then my phone rings.

Seriously? It's after nine on a school night. Gavin is getting really annoying if he's switched from texting to calling me.

But the number on the screen isn't the "contractor". It's Shawn.

My freaking ex.

The last time I spoke to him was when he was breaking up with me. I cried, and he apologized. He ... *apologized.* He said he felt bad and that I was a really nice person. He also said he just couldn't date someone as tall as me.

I think we might have even agreed to the pathetically impossible notion of "staying friends." Of course, I knew we wouldn't. No one stays friends with their ex, especially after the ex in question starts dating a much more beautiful and shorter girl immediately after dumping you.

Still, it's kind of weird.

"Hello?" I say timidly, wondering if I should even bother talking to him.

"Hey, Rissa." His voice is easy going, laid back. Same ol' Shawn. Although I feel like telling him my name is *Clarissa* and only good friends get to shorten it like that. He dumped me, therefore we are not good friends anymore.

But I don't. Instead, I take the high road and stay civil.

"Um, what's up?"

"Not much," he says. His voice is like a slap of nostalgia straight in my face. I'm suddenly thrown back in time, talking to him in this same place in my bedroom, at this same late time, just like I did three months ago.

"So listen, Rissa, um, I just had this question."

"Okay..." I say. He almost sounds nervous, but that can't possibly be right.

"I just heard some stuff lately, and I was curious to know if you're dating Gavin Voss now?"

I nearly choke on my own spit. I'm not sure if this is hilarious or terrifying or both. "Why?" I say, smiling so it sounds like I'm not as depressed as I am. "Are you jealous?"

"So you *are* dating him?"

I snort. "Who told you that?"

"Just heard it around. Like, that ya'll are dating now or hanging out or something."

I stare up at my ceiling as I lay on my bed. This is actually funny, now that I think about it. I am almost positive he's jealous. Shawn, while totally hot and fairly popular, isn't exactly on the same rung as Gavin on the popularity ladder. He's probably several steps below. So even though I hate Gavin, Shawn clearly doesn't know that, and the opportunity to make him feel crappy in a way he's made me feel lately is just too good to pass up.

"Wow, that's so weird," I say slowly. "I mean, I'm like a nobody in that school, but I start hanging out with the famous Gavin Voss and now people are talking about me."

"So, you *are* together?"

"Shawn, I'm surprised that you even care. I mean...you broke up with me."

"I don't care. I mean, it's not a big deal, Rissa. I just heard some stuff and I was curious. I'm actually dating someone now, too, so it's all good."

I take a shuddering breath. I know he has a girlfriend, but hearing him say it just hurts me in this weird way. It shouldn't. And I'm over him. And it's all old freaking news. But it still hurts. I still feel rejected, not good enough, and worst of all, I feel pathetically, freakishly tall.

Maybe if things were different, and if Gavin hadn't been a massive douchebag who lied to me, then maybe I'd feel on top of the world right now. If things were still good with him like they'd been that night we went on a date, maybe I'd laugh at Shawn and let him know how wonderfully happy I am. But that's not life, not now, not for me.

"Well, if you're happy then I'm happy for you, Shawn." It's the fakest voice I've ever had, but he seems to buy it.

"Thanks, Rissa. I'm happy for you, too. Gavin is a cool guy and he's like really tall so he's good for you."

I grit my teeth together. God forbid you date someone because you *like* them, not because of their height. Instead of telling him off, I force myself to laugh. "I don't know what rumors you heard, but I'm not dating Gavin. I mean, hooking up with someone isn't commitment, you know?"

I feel so dirty saying it, talking like I'm this badass girl who dates around and doesn't get her heart broken. But I want him to feel a little tug of jealously, the same tug I get when I see him with Mindy.

"Cool, cool," he says quickly. "I feel you."

"Good talk," I say, and then I tell him goodbye.

My hands shake as I put the phone down and let my mind replay that stupid conversation a million times. Shawn clearly has old information about me and Gavin. Or maybe Gavin just hasn't told any of his friends that I hate him now. If he couldn't tell me the truth, then he probably lies to his friends too. He probably lies to everyone.

Even an hour after that phone call is over, I'm still in bed, staring hopelessly at the ceiling. My life feels like a roller-coaster lately. First, I was so happy with Shawn, my first real boyfriend. Then he dumped me, and I went swooping down that metaphorical roller coaster. Then Grandpa and I built the greenhouse and I felt better about myself. I had a purpose and a mission. Then it was destroyed. Another hill on the roller coaster.

Then that date with Gavin brought me up the tracks to

the peak of happiness. It was only about twenty four hours, but they were the best. I liked him so much it hurt.

And then it all came crashing down again.

But my life isn't a roller coaster, no matter how much it may feel like one. In life, there's no guarantee you'll ever go back up again.

CHAPTER SIXTEEN

GAVIN

TUESDAY MORNING another stack of papers lands on my desk. I barely got any sleep last night because my dad went on another drinking spree and stayed up all night shouting about money. So it's probably because of my exhaustion that I don't register who hands me the papers at first.

"Hey," I say quickly, snapping my head up to look at Clarissa while she's still facing my direction.

She nods to the papers, and that's the only form of acknowledgement I get. I flip through them and see that they're blueprints, printed off some website called Easy Greenhouse Construction.

"This is everything we need," she says. "I can bring all of the tools."

"Tools?" I flip through the papers, grateful that they make some kind of sense to me. I'm not a carpenter, but I can read instructions. This doesn't look too hard.

"Saw, hammers. That kind of thing."

It's the most she's talked to me since we went on that date. I try to smile. "Sounds good. I can't wait to get started."

"When will that be, exactly?" She's staring at me now, like she's finally decided to acknowledge that I exist, but the quirk in her lip tells me she could change her mind any second. I'm sitting in my desk and she's still standing, hovering over me, her eyebrows taut and lips pressed together.

"Soon," I say, realizing that's not a good enough answer. *Right freaking now*, is what I wish I could say. *Let's blow off school and spend the day together.* Instead, I quickly think over my schedule.

"Wednesday. I'm off work so we can start right after school."

"That's tomorrow," Clarissa says. "Do you mean tomorrow or next Wednesday?"

She's so mean it's almost sexy. "Tomorrow," I stammer. This girl's got me all flustered. I hate thinking it, but I'm still holding out hope that she'll decide to give me another chance. "Sorry, I meant tomorrow."

Her expression softens a little. "Then why didn't you just say tomorrow?"

I shrug.

She swallows and then sinks into her chair. "Tomorrow then," she says, and then she turns toward the front of the class and continues to ignore me.

That conversation with Clarissa haunts me while I'm at work. The second I'd walked in the door of Magic Mark's, my boss had pulled me aside and asked if I could come into work tomorrow. I told him no, and he seemed annoyed, but he let it go.

But now, I've had to listen to two voicemails from my mom and I'm wondering what the hell I should do. After my next delivery, I park back at the pizza shop, pull out my phone, and play the messages again.

"Honey, it's Mom. Your dad's not going to tell you this, but he was laid off from work two days ago. He told me I wasn't allowed to tell you, but I am, so please keep this between us. I know I said I wouldn't borrow money from you again, but if you have any to spare, we could really use it. I love you, Gavin. Call me back."

The second one is much shorter.

"Hey, sweetie! It's Mom again. I know you're busy at work but can you call me ASAP?"

I dig in my pocket and pull out the wad of cash I've received in tips tonight. Twenty six bucks. I know there's around a hundred left at home and my paychecks are much higher now that I'm working five days a week. I'll get paid on Friday, so I add it all up in my head, minus the money I need for gas. Then I call my mom.

"Gavin! I'm so sorry I kept bothering you."

"Mom, it's fine. I don't mind."

"Did you listen to my voicemail messages?"

"Yeah. How the hell did Dad get fired?"

She sighs. "Apparently he just wasn't working hard enough. Probably because he goes to work hungover every damn morning. Honey, I don't even know. I'm trying to pick up extra shifts but they don't want me going over thirty-nine hours a week. I even put up an ad on Facebook saying I can clean houses on my days off."

I grit my teeth. My mom already works her ass off at her

job and at home, taking care of us and the house. She doesn't need a second job.

"How much money do you need?" I ask.

Another sigh. "Just anything you can spare."

I stare into the storefront of Magic Mark's as I talk on the phone. Inside, Pete, my boss, is running around like a crazy person. He usually spends his shifts sitting on his ass while the teenage employees do all the work, but Jayson's mom is in the hospital and our other pizza maker, Zoey, just came down with mono.

They could really use me tomorrow, and it would give me more money to help out my family. But working tomorrow would mean I'd have to cancel my plans with Clarissa.

"I have about a hundred dollars right now," I say. "And then I get paid on Friday. Is Dad already looking for another job?"

"Yes," she says softly. "You know how he is."

Dad is a pathetic drunk, but he's also a good worker. He's been fired or laid off a few times in life, but he's always found another job right away. Lately, his drinking has been worse than ever, but I have to believe that he'll find his way back.

"We'll be fine, Mom. He'll get a new job."

"I know," she says, and her voice cracks. I press my ear to the phone and I can hear her crying. The sound breaks my heart. I can't remember the last time I saw my mom cry, or if I ever have seen her cry.

"We're not going to make the mortgage payment," she says, still sobbing. "I don't know what we're going to do."

"It's okay," I say, but even I don't have much faith in my words. "Don't they take like three months of missed payments before they start to foreclose on you?"

I hate that I know this fact about mortgages, but I do.

"Yes, Gavin. But this will be our third late payment."

My stomach clenches. Shit. Things are worse than I thought. As a kid, my parents would argue about money, but then my dad would pull through and get some great job and we'd be fine again. I never really worried about it, but now I'm a few months away from being eighteen and it's all I can worry about. I don't want to hear my mom cry anymore. I don't want my dad to drink himself stupid every night because he's stressed about not having enough money.

For the first time in my life, I feel like I can make a difference. "Mom, it'll be fine. I'm working extra shifts and I'll have more money. It's all yours."

"Gavin, I can't ask you to do that," she says, her voice still broken up from crying.

"You're not asking," I say, knowing this decision won't win me any favors from Clarissa. "I'm insisting."

I wait until the next day at school to tell Clarissa the bad news. She walks into homeroom right before the bell rings, which is her new routine. I tap her on the shoulder.

"Bad news," I say.

She turns around, one eyebrow lifted. I'm surprised how much I don't want to tell her something disappointing. I had thought about texting her instead, but this way is better.

"I'm really sorry, but I got called into work tonight."

She just stares at me, as if she's waiting for me to continue. She's going to make me tell her in detail that I'm cancelling our plans. I swallow. "It's one of those situations where I can't get out of it. Can we start the greenhouse next week?"

"What day next week?" she asks after a nerve-racking few seconds of silence.

"I'm not sure," I admit. "I don't know the schedule yet."

"Tell me when you do." She turns back around, leaving me feeling like shit. I wish I could tell her that I'm working to save my family and if that weren't the case, I'd be there in a heartbeat. I'd never bail on her if I had any other choice. But my old soccer friends are in the next row over, just waiting to hear me say something they can mock, and the teacher is walking to the front of the class, and there's just no time. I'll explain everything to her later.

And that's what I keep telling myself as I'm forced to bail on her for the next three weeks.

CHAPTER SEVENTEEN

Clarissa

LIVI USES her thumbnail to scratch her name into the Styrofoam cup of her smoothie. It's Five Dollar Friday at our local smoothie place, and we decided to order the large size for just five bucks instead of the usual ten. It was kind of a mistake because this thing is unbelievably huge.

"I thought I loved smoothies, but I'm not sure I love them this much," I say, curling my lip as I stare at what's left of mine.

"Why do they even *make* them this big?" she says, but then she takes another sip. "Soo good... Maybe that's why."

I laugh and kick out my foot to make the porch swing sway a little harder. It's Friday night and we're officially two losers who have nothing better to do than get oversized smoothies and drink them on my front porch.

I heave a big, bored sigh.

"We need a car," she says.

"Agreed." I don't earn enough money to buy my own car. But now that Grandpa won't be driving his truck anymore, I keep thinking that maybe I could drive it from now on. I haven't mentioned it to him yet because his blindness is still fresh and I know he hates admitting that he can't do everything anymore. Giving up his truck would be a big loss for him. But maybe someday, I can use it on a regular basis and then I can say goodbye to the school bus.

"Thanks for hanging out with me even though I'm boring as hell," I say with a little laugh.

"*I'm* the boring one," Livi says. "I don't even know anything we could do, even if we had cars. It's not like we have boyfriends or anything." She stops talking abruptly. "Shit, I shouldn't have said that."

I shrug. "We never have boyfriends, Liv."

"I know but..." she looks at me like I'm supposed to know what she's talking about. When I don't, she says it slowly. "The...Gavin thing...?"

"Oh," I say with a snort. "He's not a thing."

In fact, he's nothing.

He was a brief date so long ago that I've already forgotten about it. And then he was a promise that he quickly broke.

I grit my teeth and inhale through my nose, then slowly exhale. "Ugh, I haven't even thought about him lately."

"Really?" Livi sets her smoothie down on the porch. "I just figured you didn't want to talk about him."

"There's nothing to talk about anymore. He promised to help me build the greenhouse and then he just kept bailing on me. Now he can go fall into a hole for all I care."

That first week I'd had my hopes up. Every day I went to homeroom and asked if he could start construction after school. Every day he said no because he was busy, or worse—he said maybe. The maybes always turned into nos. I'm sure he has some pathetic excuse, but I never wanted to hear it.

He's just an asshole. I've made his life easier for him by just forgetting the whole freaking ordeal.

Now, I have a plan. I go to homeroom just before the bell rings. I sit in my chair and look straight ahead, and then I leave the second the dismissal bell rings. It's a brilliant system. It lets me just pretend he doesn't even exist anymore, which is good for my fragile heart.

"He hasn't even been to school much lately," I say, hating that I know that. He's missed every Friday for the last three weeks, and even when he's in school, I never see him at his lunch table anymore. Not that I'm looking.

"So, your greenhouse?" Livi says softly. "Is it over?"

"Yeah," I say after a long moment. "I guess it is."

CHAPTER EIGHTEEN

GAVIN

SOON. I had promised her soon. And now it's October. Even though I see her every day in homeroom, for those fifteen minutes it's like she doesn't exist and I don't exist, at least not in the same universe. She ignores me, like she should. She should never talk to me again. She should forget my name and forget my face and forget that one perfect night we spent together.

Of course, just because she *should* doesn't mean I want her to. It's already been established that I'm a shitty person, and I've only made myself more shitty by going to work every possible day instead of helping her rebuild the greenhouse. A layer of tall grass now wraps around the supplies on the ground between the high school and the daycare. It's been weeks and I haven't had time to help her.

I know she won't talk to me, and I don't blame her one bit, but I have to explain. I have to let her know. So I write a letter.

It takes me several hours over several days. I sit up in my bed well past bedtime and write until the early morning hours. I toss out a dozen drafts before I finally settle on one. I owe her an explanation, and an apology. She doesn't have to read it, but I write as neatly as possible in the hopes that she will.

Clarissa,

If you've opened this letter, I hope you'll read it all. I owe you an apology. I owe you more than an apology. I have no explanations for what I've done, only piss poor excuses and the pleading hope that you'll someday forgive me.

I want to explain.

The first day of school went by in a blur. I'd barely slept the night before thanks to my dad going on another one of his drinking binges, so I barely paid attention in any of my classes, especially homeroom. My feet were on your desk because all I wanted to do was kick back and go to sleep. Even in a busy classroom filled with twenty people all talking at once, it was more serene than trying to sleep at my house with one raging alcoholic.

When school was over, I went home to more of the same bullshit. Exhaustive, depleting bullshit. I was in a mood. This doesn't excuse anything, I know. One of my teammates, and up until now, a guy I considered my friend, was drunk and most likely high and decided to wreak havoc on the first thing he found. That was your greenhouse.

I tried to stop him. I tried to stop myself. But months of exhaustion and stress all came out at once and suddenly I was helping him. I swear to God, I thought the greenhouse belonged to the school. I figured the school didn't care. I also thought it wasn't being used since it's been sitting there vacant for as long as I could remember.

In the dark, I didn't see that it was new. In the daylight, I could see that very well. Had I realized we weren't destroying an old shack, I probably would have stopped.

The reason I never came forward was fear. Fear of what would happen to me when my dad found out that I'd destroyed someone's private property. So I kept quiet. I focused on the girl in homeroom who was so beautiful she made my head spin. All I wanted was to get to know you. I wanted to take my mind off every other shitty thing in my life and spend my time with you.

So I kept lying. But only about the greenhouse. Everything else, every word, was true.

I know I promised to rebuild your greenhouse, and I haven't been around much lately. My promise is valid. My timing is off.

My dad has lost his job and my parents need help with the bills. I have taken on as many work hours as possible to bring in money for them, and that leaves no more time left to build the greenhouse. I'm even ditching school on Fridays so I can work sixteen hours straight. I know this isn't a good enough excuse. I know I've lost your trust and your friendship. I just wanted you to know the truth, Clarissa. I screwed up when I took a hammer to that greenhouse, and I screwed up worse when I lied to you. And that friend who got me into this trouble has now taken an interest in you, which is something I'll never forgive myself for. Now, abandoning you with the rebuilding efforts is the last thing I want to be doing, trust me. I spend every day thinking about the day when I'll be able to help. I hope it's soon. Please don't give up on me. I will build this greenhouse for you.

I'm sorry for everything.

Gavin

It's the best I can do. I fold up the letter and put it in an envelope, and then seal the envelope shut. I've revealed my worst secrets in here, and I don't want anyone to accidently read it.

In the morning, I slip past my dad, who is passed out on the couch wearing the same clothes he wore yesterday. Mom isn't home yet because she went straight from work to cleaning someone's house. I make a sandwich and grab some snack food from the pantry and shove it all in a plastic shopping bag. I've been eating my lunch in my truck now. I can't afford to go out and I'm no longer welcome at the lunch table with my old soccer friends. I could probably make more friends, but I have no energy for that.

At school, I tuck my letter under the cover of my chemistry book, which I place on my desk in homeroom. I wait patiently for Clarissa to arrive, just a few seconds before the bell, just like always.

She's wearing tight jeans and a black sweater that has a cat face on the front. She's adorable, as always. She slips into her chair, and for the first time in weeks, I don't look away.

I sit up straight. Reach into my chemistry book. I lean forward, my hand reaching out to tap her on the shoulder.

Then TJ beats me to the punch. "Hey, girl." He slides his desk halfway across the aisle so that he's closer to her as he leans over, laying on a heavy smile.

"Good morning," she tells him, her voice sweet. It's the kind of voice she hasn't used on me in a long time.

He gives her a quick once-over that makes my skin crawl. A knot twists in my stomach as I watch this event happing right in front of me, by two people who don't even notice I'm here.

"What are you up to tonight?" TJ asks her.

She shrugs. "Absolutely nothing," she says, and maybe it's my imagination but it's almost like she's flirting. The knot in my stomach gets tighter. TJ knows I went out with her. He knows I like her. Why would he do this after he's already taken everything else from me? Because of him, I'm off the team, I'm out several hundred dollars, and Clarissa hates me.

The homeroom teacher begins her morning speech, talking about upcoming events and shit I never listen to. TJ holds up a finger to Clarissa, signaling that their conversation will continue soon.

I sit so still my vision blurs as I stare straight ahead, hoping I'm wrong in my assumptions. As soon as the announcements are over, the teacher hands a stack of papers to some guy on the front row and he begins passing them out.

TJ taps Clarissa on the arm. "You wanna get dinner tonight?"

Dammit.

She seems to consider it a moment. I expect her to ask him a bunch of questions, but all she says is, "Sure."

"Sweet. Can I get your number?" TJ holds out a pen, and then puts his arm in her lap. Anger rolls around in the pit of my stomach. This is not happening.

She takes his hand and writes her number on his forearm.

Every second that passes is like another knife being stabbed into my back. I'm right here. I see all of this.

And he knows it.

"I'll call you later," TJ promises, sealing the deal with a wink.

I see her cheeks turn pink just before the bell rings. I bolt out of that classroom like it's on fire. What the hell is this shit? He's doing it to piss me off, he has to be. TJ doesn't go for girls like Clarissa. He likes them slutty. Drunk girls at parties. Freshmen. He doesn't like sweet girls like Clarissa.

I don't even realize what I'm doing at first. My feet take me down to the math hallway. As soon as she turns the corner, I release the breath I'd been holding. She's alone. That dickhead didn't follow her to her next class. This is my chance.

She doesn't even see me because she's looking down at her phone. I step in front of her.

"You can't go out with him."

She startles, then looks at me with hatred in her eyes. "Excuse you?"

"TJ is a dick. You can't go out with him."

"I can go out with whoever I want," she says, stepping to the side.

"Yeah, but dating him would be a mistake."

"Good thing I have experience in dating mistakes," she snaps.

I sigh. "Please, Clarissa. Don't do it."

She just glares at me. There are so many things I wish I could say, but even if she'd listen, there's not enough time between classes. That's when I remember the letter. I pull it out of my book and hand it to her. "Just read this. Please."

"What is it?" she says, turning over the blank envelope."

"It's a letter from me."

She rolls her eyes. That cuts me worse than a knife.

"Hate me all you want, but TJ will only hurt you."

"I'm sorry, I can't find a reason to believe anything you say." She shoves my letter into her binder and then grips it to her chest. At least she didn't rip it up on sight.

"Just read the letter," I say. "Please."

She turns toward her classroom and doesn't bother looking me in the eye anymore. "Don't tell me what to do."

I stand there for a second, my muscles rebelling against any movement. I'm overwhelmed with being in her presence again. I'm relieved that I finally gave her the letter, and even though she hates me, she might read it. If she reads it, maybe she'll find a way to forgive me.

Or maybe I've already lost her to TJ.

CHAPTER NINETEEN

Clarissa

I'M NOT sure if there's two date-worthy outfits in my closet. I'd worn the best one I had when I went on a date with a guy that I no longer think about. At least I try not to think about him. Somehow he's always in my head.

TJ texted me half an hour ago asking if I still wanted to get dinner with him. I said yes, and he said cool, and I'm still waiting on more details. I stare in my closet while wearing my underwear and a bra, hoping that a perfect date night outfit will magically appear. Maybe it'll fly off the hangers and slide onto my body, Cinderella style.

When nothing happens, I sit on my bed and text TJ again.

Me: Where are we going?

TJ: Lone Star Diner. Only the best food on the planet

. . .

Okay, that makes it easier. The diner is a small place in town and dressing up for it is definitely not required. I think it's cool that he's keeping our date low-key, although I can't imagine a romantic walk along Main Street afterward would be as fun as a walk on the beach. Not that it matters, I remind myself. That date with Gavin was a sham.

I choose an outfit and don't second guess myself as I get dressed. This is laid back and casual. It's how normal teenagers date. I put my phone on silent and slip it in my purse and then go to wait for TJ on the porch. The last thing I want is for my grandpa to meet another boy. He may not be able to see, but he still remembers everything and I'd hate to answer why I'm suddenly going out with a different guy so soon after the first.

When I step outside, TJ is already here, parked on the side of the road in his silver SUV. I wave at him and walk to the car.

"I didn't know you were here," I say, climbing inside.

"I was just about to text you." He puts the car in gear and starts driving. "You look hot."

"Thanks," I say, buckling my seatbelt. I wish first dates weren't a thing, because they're so awkward. Why can't everyone just skip ahead to the third or fourth date where you know the person better?

As we drive to the diner, there's not much to say, so the conversation is stilted. TJ's radio fills the silence, and I'm so grateful that we're only traveling a few blocks to the diner. It hits me now that I don't really know this guy at all. We've had a few conversations in homeroom about nothing important, and I know he's on the soccer team. That's it.

I do feel a little guilty because I haven't told my mom or

Livi or anyone about this date. I just lied to Mom and said I had dinner plans with friends, and I didn't tell Livi anything.

A part of me wonders if this is because of Gavin's warning. Am I scared that he's right? I screwed up big time by telling my mom and Livi about my date with Gavin because now they know it didn't work out. I won't make that mistake again. I'm keeping this date to myself until I know it will lead to something more.

The diner is busy for a Monday night, and I recognize a few people as we make our way inside, though I'm not close friends with anyone.

"Ladies first," TJ says, motioning with his arm as we make our way to a booth in the back. I smile and sit down.

"I'm glad you came out with me," TJ says. He grins at me from across the cozy two-seater booth. He's cute, with dark eyes and light hair, and a somewhat stocky build. TJ is like most guys, which means he's not taller than I am, but maybe an inch or so shorter.

"Thanks for asking me," I say.

"Order anything you want. It's on me."

I grin. "How gentlemanly of you."

TJ snorts. "That's not exactly what I'm known for, but I'll take it."

When I give him a questioning look, he winks at me. I decide to let it go. He was probably joking, but he almost seemed like he was bragging at the idea of not being a gentleman. You'd think most guys would want to be called that.

Okay, I really thought getting Gavin out of my head would be easier once I went on a date. Instead, the reverse is proving true.

TJ and I both order cheeseburgers, which are the best

thing the diner sells. He talks about soccer a lot and I pretend to care about the sport.

"Thank God we're off drills every day," he says, shoving a fry in his mouth.

"What are drills?" I ask because I haven't heard that term about soccer before.

"Exercises," he says, taking another fry. "Like, extreme exercises. We usually do them maybe fifteen minutes before practice, but Coach had us doing two hours of the shit before Gavin got caught."

I lift an eyebrow. "Why?"

"Punishment," he says. "Coach knew someone on the team messed up that shed thing and he was punishing us until someone confessed. Luckily, that bastard got caught or we'd still be doing drills."

My chest clenches. This is exactly the topic I didn't want to talk about. "It was a greenhouse," I find myself saying, despite not wanting to talk about it.

"Huh?"

"The shed he destroyed. It was a greenhouse that the daycare uses to plant flowers for the kids."

He shrugs. "Yeah, whatever it was. He's so damn stupid. Glad he got caught."

"I thought you were friends with him?" I ask, tilting my head. I know there's tension now because they don't talk in homeroom anymore, but I want to hear him explain it. Seems like Gavin ruined more than the greenhouse. He ruined his chances with me and he lost his friends.

TJ shrugs. "We were teammates so that made us friends. But now he's kicked off the team so we're not really friends anymore. Plus, he's the prick who quit coming around."

"What do you mean?" I ask.

"Parties, hanging out. Hell, he doesn't even sit with us at lunch anymore."

"Looks like he isolated you first."

TJ nods. "Hell yeah he did. Why so much Gavin talk?" he asks, peering at me over narrow eyes. "You still like him or something?"

Oh God, I think I'm blushing now. "I do not like Gavin," I say, trying to keep my voice level. "Not in any way."

"Yeah, well you used to," he says. His lips turn into the tiniest smirk. "Did you two date or something?"

Something in this eyes tells me he probably already knows the answer. I shrug, trying to act just as casual as he is. "We hung out, like once."

"And why not twice?"

"He ruined my greenhouse."

"Your greenhouse?" TJ asks, lifting a brow.

I'm trying to have a nice time here, so I don't bother bringing up the importance of it. "I work at the daycare," I say as an explanation.

He nods. "Well this date has had enough talk of idiots in it. Let's move to a new topic. You like hiking?"

"Sure," I say, which is about as true as I can answer since I've never been hiking. Maybe I do like it. "Why?"

"There's a cool trail along that man-made lake off Northpoint." He reaches for the bill on our table and lays some cash on top of it. "You want to go?"

I check the time. "Sure, but I need to get home around nine. My hair doesn't look this amazing unless I spend two hours washing and drying it."

TJ just stares at me because I guess he doesn't get my

joke. Gavin would have laughed, said something silly back to me. *Or maybe even complimented my hair*, I think as my stomach gets all tingly and nervous. Gavin was a better conversationalist than TJ. But none of that matters anymore.

We head out to the park which is a few miles away. I've never been here because it's supposed to be a dog park and I don't have a dog. But there is a playground for kids and also a lake with a walking trail around it.

TJ takes my hand the second we step on the trail. I feel my heart clench and my breath get shallow. It's as if this hand holding thing is supposed to trigger something in me, awaken some butterflies or something. But nothing happens.

I'm not even nervous. I kind of just want to go home.

I take a deep breath and look over at TJ and smile. He smiles back. "I wish there was something more exciting to do, but this is fun too."

"We can get to know each other," I suggest. "Tell me stuff about you."

He shrugs. "Not much to tell."

We keep walking and holding hands and it's starting to get weird. I mean, no one is talking. It's just silent, save for the sound of the birds and the occasional slapping of feet as a jogger runs by us with their dog running next to them. Only a few people are at the park this late, and it's kind of the perfect romantic spot to take a walk.

But I'm so not feeling it.

Am I broken now? Did Shawn and Gavin break me? This is a freaking date. It's supposed to be fun.

We're nearly back to the start of the trail after about thirty minutes of walking in a winding circle around the small lake. I release a breath slowly, glad that we're finally about to be done with this weird date. It wasn't exactly bad, it just wasn't very fun.

I look over at him. "Does it bother you that I'm so tall?"

He shakes his head. "Nah. Why?"

"It bothers most guys."

"I'm not most guys," he says, grinning at me. That makes me feel a little better. He's already better than Shawn was. Now I just need to find a way that he's better than Gavin and maybe I can move on. Maybe I can get out of this funk and have a real boyfriend.

"So," TJ says, coming to a stop. "I think it's time for this."

"For wha—" I say, only to have my words crushed by TJ's lips. His hands grab my hips and tug me closer and then his lips are all over mine, moving and opening and closing as his tongue slithers all around my mouth. It's quick and sloppy and feels like he's about to get on a jet and blast into orbit and never see another girl again.

I realize my hands are just hanging limply at my sides, so I put them on his back. He tugs me closer and keeps kissing me for what feels like forever.

There are no fireworks.

There are no tingles in my toes.

This is a bad kiss.

And although I'm trying very hard to make the best of this, to find something to like about TJ besides the fact that he likes me, I can only focus on one stupid thing.

My date with Gavin was so much better than this.

CHAPTER TWENTY

GAVIN

I WAKE up to the smell of pancakes and syrup. Mom likes warm syrup so she microwaves it and it makes the entire house smell amazing. Breakfast foods always take me back to my childhood when we'd sit together as a family and eat every morning. Mom didn't work nights back then, so she'd be well rested and still in her pajamas. She loves cats, so most of them were covered in pictures of cats. Dad and I used to go shopping for her birthday and we'd always get her another pair of cat pajamas if we could find them.

I stretch my arms out and yawn as I make my way to the kitchen. It's Wednesday, and I don't know how, but I've successfully survived three more days of being the front row audience member of TJ hitting on my girl in homeroom. The thought of enduring one more day of this shit—the hand touching, the flirting, the stupid jokes he makes that aren't even funny—ugh, I don't know if I can do it.

Yesterday I wore earbuds to drown it out, but I'd have needed a freaking blindfold to avoid all of it. He's all over her. She seems to like it, too. It blows my mind how she'd fall for a guy like that asshat after dating me. TJ and I couldn't be more opposite.

And I know we only had one date, so it's not like we *dated*, dated. And I know she's not my girl. But in my heart, she is. At least I want her to be.

I don't know if she's read my letter or not. I have to believe that she hasn't, because I revealed some pretty embarrassing and heartfelt shit in there and I don't think she's so cruel as to ignore that.

"I love pancakes," I say. I give Mom a quick hug to let her know she's appreciated. She's wearing her Wal-Mart uniform, not her cat pajamas, and there's dark circles under her eyes.

"Pancakes are the miracle breakfast food. You know why?" she asks. I hold out my plate and she layers on some pancakes and then hands me a cup filled with warm syrup.

"Why?" I ask.

"They're cheap as hell," she says with a snort. She taps the box of pancake mix. "Only two bucks and it lasts a while."

"Oh, that reminds me." I set my food on the table and then take out my wallet. I fish for some cash and hold it out to her.

She takes it, turning it over in her hands. "It's Wednesday. You don't get paid until Friday."

"I delivered to some really rich and drunk people last night. They tipped me a hundred dollars."

"Wow," she says. "Can you imagine having that kind of money?"

I shake my head. "I even questioned them to make sure they didn't accidently hand me the hundred instead of like a ten or something. They said nope, that was my tip. I've memorized their address so if they order again, I'm going to make sure I do the delivery."

"Nice," Mom says, shoving the cash into her pocket. "You're my little lifesaver, Gavin."

"I'm taller than you," I say.

She punches me in the arm. "You know what I mean."

"What the hell was that?" Dad says. Mom and I both jump. It's seven in the morning and Dad is never awake this early if he doesn't have a job.

"Good morning," Mom says to him in that voice she uses to calm him down. It doesn't work.

His nostrils flare. "What did you just give her?"

I shrug. "Some extra cash I had."

"We don't need your money," Dad spits out.

"Honey," Mom says, her voice stern. "Yes, we do. We are desperate for more money and Gavin is just trying to help."

"What, you think you're the man of the house now?" Dad walks up to me, getting right in my face. He's a couple inches shorter than I am, but I'm embarrassed to admit that I still fear him. The hairs on the back of my neck stand up and my hands clench nervously at my side. He's my dad, not some random drunk. And he terrifies me.

"I'm just helping," I say, trying not to sound like a wimp.

He snickers. "You're a kid. This is my house. You're not the boss."

"I never said I was," I say, taking half a step back to get away from the rancid smell of his breath. "I'm just helping Mom."

"*I* will help your mother," he says, jabbing a finger into my chest. It hurts but I stand tall and refuse to wince. "*I* am the husband and the father and *I* am the man around here. You're just a dumb kid, you got that?"

Behind him, Mom pleads at me with her eyes. She doesn't want me to make this worse. Normally I'd agree with her, but I can't keep my mouth shut.

I stand to my full height and peer down at my father. "At least I have a job."

He hisses. Takes a step back. "You think some after school minimum wage job makes you a man? You're just a kid."

He whirls around to face my mother and points an angry finger at her. I rush forward and grab his arm, yanking it back. "Get away from her. She's more of a man than you are, Dad. She works her ass off and she keeps our bills paid. All you do is drink your life away."

The slap is hard, quick, and painful. Right across my face.

I blink, unable to interpret for a second. My dad slapped me across the face. I guess that's better than a punch.

"Get away from us," I say, stepping between him and Mom.

"You telling me what to do?" There's an angry bulging vein in his forehead.

I nod once.

"You can't tell me what to do, son!"

I hold up my hand and cut off whatever tirade he's about to go on. "I can. You know why? Because I'm sober. I'm responsible. I'm helping Mom keep our house afloat, keeping food on the table, keeping your precious cable TV connected. And you know what you are?" I say, my voice getting angrier by the moment. "You're a jobless drunk. You smell like garbage and body odor and you're a complete waste of space. You call yourself a husband and father but you're just a drain on the family. You're not a man in any way. You're an embarrassment."

Dad looks like I've just slapped him across the face, maybe even worse than that, because I'm the one who got slapped and I'm not showing it. His eyes flit to me and Mom, who is shaking as she stands behind me. He swallows, and then turns around.

Mom and I stand in silence as we watch him grab his cell phone and car keys and then rush out the front door, letting it slam closed behind him. A moment later, his truck starts up and he drives away.

"Where do you think he's going?" I ask.

Mom lowers her head and stares at the now burnt pancake on the stove. "I don't know."

I'm changing into my Magic Mark's red polo shirt when Mom calls me. I grab my keys and flip off the light in my bedroom. As I predicted, today was another day of misery in homeroom class, only it got worse because I saw TJ walking with Clarissa in the hallway between two classes, despite my best efforts to avoid them. This day has been a complete nightmare and now I'm headed off to work, which I'm growing really sick of.

As I'm making my way out to the car, I answer the phone. "Hello?"

"Gavin." Mom's voice is weird. I stop on the front porch, my hand holding the key in the lock.

"Yeah?"

"Guess what?"

"We won the lottery?"

"Not quite, but close."

I lift an eyebrow. "You sound happy."

"I *am* happy. Your dad just called me. He got his roofing job back."

"He did *what?*"

Mom laughs. "Can you believe it? That's where he went this morning when he left. He went straight back to his boss and begged for his job back. And guess what? His boss agreed to rehire him but only if he attends AA meetings."

"You're kidding me," I say.

She laughs again. "He just called me and said he spent the day working. He told me he's not too happy about the AA thing but he's going to at least try it."

"Wow... I ... don't know what to say." This is surreal. Dad actually got his job back. He agreed to attend Alcoholics Anonymous meetings. Is this real life?

"I know, honey. I feel such a huge relief. Maybe Dad can get the help he needs, you know?"

"Yeah," I say, turning around when I hear the sound of a car engine. Dad pulls into the driveway. "He's here. I gotta go."

"Try to be nice, Gavin. He's trying."

"I will," I promise. "Have a good night at work."

I step off the porch and start walking toward my truck. It's impossible to avoid Dad because the driveway is only so big. He gets out of his truck.

"Gavin," he says.

I open my truck door and peer at him. "Dad."

He frowns. In the sunlight, he looks older than usual, with dark circles under his eyes and wrinkles I haven't seen before. "Son, I'm sorry about this morning."

"It's okay." I don't know why I say it, because it's not okay, not really.

He shakes his head. "I'm sorry for a lot of things."

I nod. I don't think I've ever heard him apologize before.

He sighs. "I got my job back. I'm gonna keep it this time. I promise you."

I nod again. "That's good."

"Yeah." He gives me a flat sort of smile and then scrubs his hand across his face. "I'm tryin' kid." Another sigh. "I'm gonna try."

That might be the most heartfelt thing he's ever told me. I meet his gaze. "Thank you, Dad."

The whole drive to work feels like I'm living in someone else's life. Someone with a little luck and hope in their future. I keep grinning for no reason when I think about what my dad told me in the driveway, how happy Mom sounded on the phone. Dad getting a job was important but the AA meetings might actually save him. This might be the start of something good for my family. Maybe Dad can heal from his addiction and become a real dad again.

And that's making me think that maybe other things can heal, too. When I get to work, I head straight to Pete's office.

"Do you think I could have the weekend off work?"

He shrugs. "Sure. You've been working your ass off lately."

"I don't think I have to do that anymore," I say.

"Oh yeah? You got free time now?" he says, though I

know he doesn't really care. He just wants to get back to the game he's playing on the computer.

I nod anyway. "Yeah. In fact, I think I'm going to help a friend with something I've been needing to do for a long time."

CHAPTER TWENTY-ONE

Clarissa

IT IS a glorious day in the daycare world. Our worn-out Frozen DVD has now been overtaken by a much better movie. After years of the kids begging to watch Frozen, and years of wanting to superglue earplugs into my ears to avoid hearing those dumb songs, the movie has been dethroned. Moana is now all the rage, and I totally love it.

Don't get me wrong, I'm sure I'll grow to hate the movie eventually. There's only so many times you can watch the same thing at work each day. But for some reason the kids love the repetition.

While the dozen toddlers are all laying on the big circle rug and watching the movie, I prepare twelve cups of juice and twelve plates with crackers, cheese, and grapes on them for snack time. I love being at work because it helps me take my mind off things.

Lately, things at home are a little hard to get used to. Grandpa is getting depressed from not being able to see, and it breaks my heart. He hates having to ask us for help, but he can't do most things by himself anymore. Mom is extra stressed about it, too. I've been doing what I can around the house to make both of their lives easier. And even though coming to work is usually stressful because kids are crazy and need lots of attention, lately it's been my reprieve from everything else in my life.

I gather the kids up and have them sit at the tables for their snack. In my back pocket, my phone vibrates, but I don't check it. Cell phones aren't exactly forbidden at work, but I think it's wrong to send flirty texts when I'm watching people's children.

And I know it's probably TJ texting me, because it's always TJ texting me. He's been all over me this week, walking me to class, texting me, and even sitting with me and Erin at lunch two times.

I don't know how I feel about it. I'm trying really hard to like him, and I do like him a little. But it's not like this instant love connection. He really seems to like me though, so I'm trying to get to know him better, trying to like him. I keep wondering if things would be different if I had never experienced the heartbreak from Shawn and Gavin. Would I like TJ more if my heart wasn't already hurt?

Mrs. Bradley comes into the toddler room a second later, and I'm glad I didn't take out my phone to check the text. Now I still look like a model employee. She smiles warmly at me.

"You wanna take off early?"

"Huh? Why would I do that?" My shift only started thirty minutes ago.

"Well, I thought you might want to help."

"Help what?"

Now she looks just as confused as I do. "Help outside? Your greenhouse?"

I run to the window and peer outside. Gavin's truck is parked in front of the greenhouse. He's moving materials around and setting them into piles.

"Wow," I say, my breath fogging the cold window. It's only October but it's been colder than usual lately. "I can't believe he's here."

Mrs. Bradley doesn't know the whole story, just that the guy who promised to help rebuild the greenhouse hasn't done it yet. I turn to her. "Would you mind?"

"Of course not," she says. "Stay on the clock since you'll still be working on the greenhouse."

I smile. "Thank you."

I don't know why I do it, but I head into the kitchen and make two mugs of hot chocolate. Then I make my way outside. It's nearly six o'clock and the sun will be setting in about thirty minutes. In the time it took me to get over here, Gavin has turned on his truck's headlights to use them as light.

My heart pounds as I get closer. He still hasn't seen me. The smell of the hot chocolate makes my mouth water and I find myself hoping he'll like it, even though I hate him and I shouldn't care. It's a special recipe that Mrs. Bradley uses and we make a big pot of it every day when it's cold. The kids love it.

Finally, Gavin looks up. His cheeks are pink from the cold, and he's only wearing jeans and a grey sweater when he really should have a jacket.

"Hi," he says, almost as if he's afraid to talk.

"Hello." I hold out one of the paper coffee cups. Steam rises from the plastic lid. "Hot chocolate," I say.

He takes one in his gloved hands. "Thank you."

I gaze over the piles of building supplies as he takes a sip. "Wow, this is good."

"I know," I say, drinking from mine. "Secret recipe."

"Clarissa I'm sorry it's taken me so long."

I look up at him, seeing nothing but desperation and worry in his eyes. He scratches the back of his neck. "Did you read my letter?"

I chew on my bottom lip, then shake my head. His letter is still sealed in the envelope. It's shoved in the drawer of my nightstand. I don't know why, but I can't bring myself to read it right now. I guess I'm afraid it'll make me stop hating him so much, and if I do that, then I'll get hurt again. I can't let myself fall for Gavin Voss another time. I just can't.

"Okay," he says. "Well, I need to get to work."

"What can I help with?" I ask.

"It's cold. Don't worry about it."

"I'm wearing warmer clothing than you are," I say, chugging another sip of my hot chocolate. I set it down on the bumper of his truck. "Let's work."

Gavin has already cut the wooden frame pieces to size. We lay them out and hammer them into individual walls, just like Grandpa and I had done this summer. As we work, we don't talk unless necessary. Like, "hand me that tape measure," or "can you get another box of nails?"

I find myself slipping into the work. Focusing on the hammer hitting the nail, the pieces lining up at the corners. After a while, I take off my jacket because even though it's cold outside, the work is warming me up.

Gavin works much faster than Grandpa did. Within an hour, we have all four walls built and we're ready to raise them. It's pretty dark outside but the headlights on his truck are keeping things lit.

"Is that going to kill your battery?" I ask after we raise one of the walls. I hold it into place while he screws it into the foundation.

"I hope not," he says.

I give him a look. He peers up at me, socket wrench in hand. From the lighting of his headlights, he looks unusually sexy. He grins.

"It'll be fine. That's a new battery."

"Good," I say, taking a deep breath. I hold his gaze longer than I should. Moments tick by and we're still here, me standing near the framed wall, and him sitting on the foundation, looking up at me.

"Next wall?" he says after a painfully long moment where all I want to do is talk to him like we used to.

"Sure," I say, my voice coming out all wrong.

He gets up and helps me position the next wall into place. A little while later, we have four standing framed walls of the greenhouse. My phone goes off in my back pocket again, but I ignore it. It makes me think of TJ's name on my phone, and how Gavin's is now saved as Contractor.

And honestly, that's exactly who he is tonight. He hasn't said a word that wasn't work related. He's just been working hard, building this thing by memory as if he'd memorized the blueprints I gave him. Every step he does is exactly in order.

"Thank you for this," I say because I'm dying to say something. Being here with him, close enough to smell his cologne, it makes me long for the old days, even though I shouldn't.

"No thanks are needed. This is my job."

Just like a contractor, I think.

"Clarissa!" Mrs. Bradley calls out from across the way. I look up and can barely see her from the dim lighting at the daycare's entrance. "Do you still need a ride home?"

I look at Gavin. "Sorry. I don't have a car," I say. "I would stay the whole time if I could.

"I can give you a ride home," he says.

"Are you sure?" I ask.

"I'd love to."

My stomach flickers with something like anxiety. I cup my hands to my mouth and call back to Mrs. Bradley, "I have a ride! Thank you though!"

She waves at me. "See you tomorrow!"

And then she's gone, and I realize we're the only two people out here. The kids have long since been picked up by their parents, and the teachers from the school next door are at home, carrying on with their lives. It's just us out here in the cold.

Gavin and I assemble the frame for the roof. The silence is killing me. I study his features to see if maybe it's killing him, too, but he doesn't ever look at me. He just focuses on the task at hand.

"Sorry I didn't read your letter," I say, just because I need something to say. I miss the old us. The jokes and the banter and the fun we had.

"It's no big deal," he says after a moment. He doesn't meet my eyes. "We should probably wait until daylight to put the roof on. It'd be safer that way."

I nod slowly. I'm not ready for the night to be over, even

though my fingers are frozen and my nose is cold and that hot chocolate was gone hours ago.

"Tomorrow?" I say.

"I have the weekend off, and if we're lucky, we can get this finished by then."

He walks around the back of his truck and lowers the tailgate. I follow him, and sit on the back of it with as much space between us as possible.

"That would be cool," I say. "But wait, isn't a cold front moving in?"

He shrugs. "It's Texas. It doesn't get that cold."

"They said it might snow." I remember hearing it on the news today while I was getting ready for school. "We should put it off until the weather is better."

"I'm done putting it off," Gavin says. He looks over at me and in the darkness, his sharp good looks make my stomach flutter. "I made you a promise and I'm following through on it as fast as I can."

I exhale. "If it's too cold, we'll need to wait."

He shakes his head. "I'm really sorry, Clarissa. This is the best I can do, and I'm doing it no matter what."

I swallow. I wish he'd continue. I wish we could have that talk he begged me to have with him weeks ago. Now it all seems so distant, so unattainable.

"Come on," he says, hopping off the tailgate. "I'll take you home."

On the short drive, the only sound is of the tires on the asphalt, and the low singing of an old rock song on his radio. My throat is filled with cotton balls and all I want to do is talk to him, but I can't find the words. When he pulls into my driveway, I turn to him and smile.

"Thanks for the ride."

"You're welcome," he says, but he's not looking at me. "Have a goodnight."

I climb out of his truck, heavy with the weight of all this regret on my chest. This is because of what he did, but I still wish it didn't have to be this way. This Gavin isn't the Gavin I used to know.

Tonight he was distant. A stranger.

He was a contractor—hired help. Not a friend.

Isn't that exactly what I wanted from him?

And yet, even though we had no fun at all and all we did was work, I can't help but think that I enjoyed these few hours with Gavin so much more than all the time I've spent with TJ this week. I should be happy when I'm with TJ, the guy who likes me and hasn't lied to me.

But instead, I only feel at peace when I'm with the guy I can't trust.

And that makes absolutely no sense at all.

CHAPTER TWENTY-TWO

GAVIN

THERE'S a new feeling in the air at my house. Maybe that's just because the living room no longer smells like whiskey since Dad's working during the day instead of drinking himself stupid on the couch. But I'm thinking it's because things are starting to look up for my family. Mom is in a great mood and Dad actually went to sleep at a reasonable hour last night so he could get up early to go to work.

I can't remember the last time my family went twenty four hours without screaming at each other. Now if only the rest of my life was coming together.

I spend a few minutes going over my homework in the morning. I have a test in English, History, and Chemistry today and I'm starting to think it's cruel and unusual punishment for teachers to always test on the same day. Fridays, no less. Fridays are supposed to be a fun pre-weekend day. My grades have slipped like crazy since I took all those extra shifts at work, but now that I'm not going to work so much, I need to get my grades back up. I'll need them for college scholarships since I can't depend on a soccer scholarship anymore.

Studying keeps my mind off Clarissa, but as soon as I'm driving to school, I'm thinking about her again. Maybe it's my imagination, but I can kind of smell the strawberry scent of her in my passenger seat from where she sat last night.

Last night was equal parts amazing and terrifying. Just being around her was like a miracle. It took every ounce of strength I had to keep my feelings tucked in close to my heart. She clearly hasn't forgiven me yet, and I'm not sure she ever will. But if there's a chance, I'm not going to ruin it by constantly asking if she wants to talk to me. I just need to keep my head down, do the work I promised her, and show her that I'm a good guy.

I repeat the words to myself as I sit in homeroom. *I am a good guy. I am a good guy.*

Because it really sucks when TJ walks into class with his arm slung around Clarissa's shoulders. Something deep inside me aches at the very sight of it. And then I notice her expression. Her lips twist and her eyes seem a little disturbed. Is she not happy that his arm is around her?

I watch her as she walks to her desk. Her gaze meets mine and she gives me the softest smile before sitting down. It makes my heart stampede around in my chest. TJ flops down in the desk to my left and promptly turns around to talk to Beau.

It sucks that I'm no longer in their friend group, but I study my Chemistry textbook and keep up the charade that I don't mind it at all. I know this saying is something my mom would have told me if I were five years old, but if they aren't my friends now, then they're not good friends to begin with.

I'm fine without them, and without my soccer team. Any team who rats out one person while letting the other person get away isn't a team I want to be a part of.

Today I actually listen to something in the announcements. Because the cold front blew in last night, there's a heavy chance of snow this weekend. They're cancelling all of the athletics activities just as a precaution.

Beau curses under his breath, says he was really looking forward to tonight's game against the Bearcats.

"Dude, at least we get an unexpected Friday night off," TJ says to him.

And then I get this weird psychic-like sense. TJ will probably ask Clarissa to hang out with him tonight since he's free.

I decide I won't let that happen.

I lean forward and tap Clarissa on her right shoulder so that she turns around with her back facing TJ.

"I'm thinking I might be able to finish the greenhouse tonight," I say.

She looks at me curiously. "Really?"

I shrug. I have no idea if that's true, I just need to talk to her before TJ does. "I think so." I bite my lip. "Okay, maybe not."

She smiles. "It's a lot of work still, but putting up the siding doesn't really take that long."

"I'll send you pictures of my progress," I say, but what I wish I was saying is: *Please come with me, I want another night with you for company.*

She watches me for a moment. "I mean, I could come by and help?"

Yes. I swallow. "If you want to, yeah. But it's supposed to be really cold so you don't have to."

"No, it's okay. I want to."

TJ's dumbass voice butts in and ruins our conversation. "What are ya'll two talking about?"

We turn to face him. "Just greenhouse stuff," I say. Clarissa doesn't say anything.

TJ's eyebrows narrow. "What?"

"The greenhouse," I say again. "I'm updating her on the progress."

Again, his face is blank. Does he not know what I'm rebuilding it? Has she not told him?

This makes sparks dance in my heart. Maybe they aren't as close as I'd feared. Clarissa would tell a guy about that kind of thing if they were really dating. But now, TJ is looking confused as hell and she's not saying a word. She's actually running her finger up and down the spiral binding of her notebook.

"What progress?" TJ says, then his confusion turns into a sneer. A warning sneer. "She already knows you vandalized the thing. What more is there to tell?"

"I'm rebuilding it," I say, my voice low. "We got a great start last night."

"We?" he turns to Clarissa. "Why'd you get him to help you? I can do it."

"He..." She looks at me before continuing. "He promised to help me rebuild it."

TJ frowns. "Well, he's not your boyfriend, now is he?"

I freeze. They can't be official. There's no way. Please, please, don't be official.

Clarissa straightens, and some of that ice cold attitude of hers comes back. "I don't have a boyfriend, but the last time I checked, a woman doesn't need a boyfriend to help her do something."

"Whoa, Clarissa," TJ says, holding up his hands. "Chill out."

The bell rings and everyone gets up to leave. Everyone except for us. TJ stands, and he glares at me as he's talking to her. "You don't need Gavin to help you build something. I'll do it."

"He's the one who promised," she says. "It's his responsibility."

I stand, too. "The job is mine, dude. Don't you remember? I was the one who wrecked the greenhouse in the first place. Not anyone else. Just *me*, according to Coach, and the principal." There's a warning in my voice. A dare, just begging him to come clean about his involvement. But I know he won't. I smirk. "That means the job is all mine. And if Clarissa wants to spend the evening with me, she's free to do so."

TJ scowls. "That's all you're ever going to be to her, Gavin. Don't get any ideas. She's mine."

"I'm no one's," Clarissa says. "God, ya'll are just a couple of cavemen."

"He's the one treating you like a piece of property," I say. "I'm the one coming through on my promise." I lower my voice and talk directly to her. "We're friends, and I'd never push you to be anything else."

"Shut up, man." TJ says. "You had your chance and you ruined it."

Anger rises up so fast inside of me that I'm not sure I can control it. I am two seconds away from doing something stupid. But I can't. Not in front of Clarissa. All I can do is leave.

I grab my backpack and storm out of the classroom, noticing one very confused homeroom teacher watching me go.

"Gavin!"

I stop at the corner of the hallway when I hear Clarissa call out my name. I'm afraid to turn around, because she could be with *him*. What if she's holding his hand? What if they're both wanting to continue the conversation about how I'm nothing but a vandal to Clarissa and that TJ is the guy who has her heart now?

I grit my teeth. Then I smell her strawberry shampoo as she rushes up next to me, grabbing my arm to get my attention. I blink, wishing she'd keep it there, but of course she doesn't.

"Gavin," she says, taking a deep breath. I glance behind her, but I don't see TJ. Thank the heavens.

"What?" I start walking.

She keeps pace with me. "Don't let TJ get to you like that. He's, *ugh*, he's such an idiot."

"You shouldn't talk about your boyfriend that way."

"He's not my boyfriend."

"It sure feels like he is."

"Gavin." She says my name like she's exhausted. "Please don't let him get to you."

I walk toward an alcove near a window to get out of the rush of students heading to their first period class. She follows me, her expression sorrowful and yet still as beautiful as ever.

"Listen, Clarissa. I know I screwed up. I know I ruined

the perfect thing we had between us, but please keep in mind that TJ used to be my friend before all of this. I know the kind of guy he is, so trust me when I say that you are too good for him." I put my hands to my chest. "You don't want me, I get it. And that's fine, but you don't need him, either."

She tilts her head and peers at me. "Did you only start helping me with the greenhouse because you're jealous of TJ?"

I snort. "You're too smart of a girl to believe something like that."

"I don't know what to believe," she says.

"I know that you don't seem too happy with him."

She stiffens. "We're just...hanging out."

"Are you trying to convince yourself or me?"

She rolls her eyes. "Gavin, it's over between us. I'm glad you're helping me with the greenhouse, but I can't trust you."

Her voice cracks, and I can see it. Right there in her eyes, those deep pools of copper, she regrets what she just said. It gives me hope like I've never had before.

"I lied to you, okay? And it was stupid. But I've never cared about anyone as much as I cared about you. If I could change your opinion of me, I would. In a heartbeat."

Her breath hitches. I have to grit my teeth to stop myself from leaning forward and kissing her. She watches me for the longest moment, and I'm certain that at any second the bell will ring and we'll be late to class.

"Ditch class with me," I say. Holy shit. I said that. I can't believe I said that.

Her eyes widen. "What? Why?"

I shrug. "Spend the day with me. I'll win you over. I'll show you that I'm better than him."

Dammit, dammit, Gavin. No. I told myself to be better than this.

She looks at the floor, and then gradually brings her gaze up to mine again. "Gavin..." I can see the regret in her eyes. Sense the thoughts in her mind that swirl around, and then eventually land on what I don't want to hear. "I can't trust you. I'm sorry."

"If you knew the real TJ, you wouldn't trust him either."

Her jaw flexes. "Yeah, well, he never lied to me."

The bell rings, and we're officially late for class. I take a deep breath. "Maybe you should read my letter."

CHAPTER TWENTY-THREE

Clarissa

I CAN'T STOP THINKING about that strange talk I had with Gavin this morning. Our words replay in my mind as I go from class to class. As much as I want to be mad at him, I can't ignore the fact that he's hurting. I could see it all over his face.

His eyes, and the pain in them, haunts me as I work on my math test. I think about it during lunch when Erin talks nonstop and doesn't seem to notice that I'm not adding to the conversation.

I've been avoiding reading his stupid letter, but I did keep it in my nightstand. I guess I've been wanting to read it, thinking that one day I might actually do it, otherwise I would have thrown it away. But I can't ever bring myself to do that.

TJ catches me in the hallways before our last class. He's all energetic like he always is at the end of the day. It's the mornings when he's sleepy and sluggish.

"Hey there," he says, grinning at me from ear to ear. "How was your day?"

"I think I passed my math test."

"Cool, cool." He goes to put his arm around my shoulders, but I conveniently have to tie my shoe. It's not even that loose, but I pull the shoelace and redo it anyway. I don't want his arm around me right now. It's so awkward. We're not together-together. I don't know what we are, but all the progress I'd made in trying to make myself like him went right out the door after that talk I had with Gavin today.

Only Gavin and I can have heartfelt talks like that. With TJ, everything is so superficial.

"You want a ride home after school?" he says.

I stand back up. "Um, no thanks."

He looks offended, so I say, "I promised my friend I'd ride the bus with her so she can tell me some crazy story about her boyfriend."

"Lame. We should hang out this weekend though, when you're done with that jackass Gavin."

I nod, but I don't really feel it. Luckily, he doesn't seem to care.

On the bus ride home, I sit alone like I usually do, and I text Livi in the hopes that it'll take my mind off Gavin.

Livi: Dude! It's totally going to snow tonight!

Me: Really?

Livi: the weather app says so. WOOT!

I switch to Gavin's text and send him a message.

. . .

Me: Apparently it's supposed to snow tonight so you should stay home and we'll work on the greenhouse another night.

Contractor: This is Texas...even when it snows, it doesn't snow that much.

Me: lol, I know but still. Just be safe and save it for another time

Contractor: if you insist

I stare at the phone for a long time, wanting to reply. But I don't have anything to say. At least not right now.

As soon as I get home, I go to my nightstand and pull out the envelope. Before I can talk myself out of it, I rip it open and take out the letter. I push my door closed and sit on the bed, and then I read Gavin's words three times to let it all sink in.

I hadn't said anything to TJ when he texted me asking if he could stop by my house to hang out before going to the diner with his friends. I just texted back *sure.*

And then I waited.

Right around seven o'clock, TJ's SUV pulls into my driveway. He's never been inside my house, and I don't plan to let him in this time. I pull on my heaviest winter coat and I meet him outside.

"Hey, beautiful," he says, his breath making puffs of white smoke in the chilly air. "You gonna invite me inside, or are we gonna freeze out here?"

I fold my hands over my chest. The air is colder than ever, a crisp winter chill. But there's no snow anywhere yet. TJ's golden hair glows from the porch light.

I stare at him so long, his smile fades away. "Well?" he says.

"Did you vandalize my greenhouse?"

The question hangs in the air for so long I start to wonder if I actually said the words out loud, or if maybe I just imagined that I did.

"No," TJ finally says, but it sounds like a question. "What makes you ask that?"

"Did you vandalize my greenhouse?" I ask again. "With Gavin?"

"What the hell has he told you?" TJ exhales through his nose, his nostrils flaring. "He's just jealous that you're mine now."

"I'm not yours," I snap. "Answer the question."

"I didn't do shit to your greenhouse. Damn." TJ rattles his car keys in his hand. "If you're gonna be a bitch, I'll just go home."

"If you're going to be a liar, you should go home."

He shuffles on his feet. "I didn't do anything."

I've never seen someone so bad at lying. "We're done," I say, taking a step backward. "Don't call me anymore, don't text me. Whatever this is, it's over."

"Clarissa, seriously?" he says, throwing his hands in the air. "Are you serious right now?"

"Yeah," I snap, turning around and walking toward my door. "Bye."

I feel a rush of adrenaline as I walk back inside my house and close the door behind me. I stood up for myself and I told off a guy and it felt great. I lean against the wall and peer out the crack of the window to watch TJ get back in his car and leave.

"What are you doing?" Grandpa asks.

I look over and find him sitting on the couch, the TV turned to the news.

"Just looking out the window," I say.

"I hear it's supposed to snow tonight," Grandpa says. "I wish I could see it."

"Maybe you can go outside and feel it."

He considers it for a moment. "That would be nice."

I smile even though he can't see me, and I squeeze his hand on my way to my bedroom. Then I call Livi and tell her every single detail of what just happened.

"Whoa," she says. "But you don't even sound upset."

"Why would I be upset?" I lay on my bed and stare at the ceiling. "I feel like a badass telling him off like that."

"Yeah, but, he was like...kind of your boyfriend."

"TJ?" I groan. "Not really."

"You've been sort of dating him for a couple weeks now," she says. "And now you find out he lied to you and he was part of the greenhouse vandalism and you're totally fine? No tears at all?"

"I guess I am fine," I say with a shrug. "I definitely don't feel sad."

"Okay, but you were devastated when you found out that Gavin had lied to you about the exact same thing."

I swallow and run my hand down my face. "That's...different."

"That's the point I'm trying to make," she says slowly. "It is different. Because you actually liked Gavin."

"I liked TJ, too," I say.

"No, no you didn't. I'm your best friend and I know these things. You *wanted* to like him but you didn't."

"Yeah, well they're both liars," I say with a sigh. "I can't deal with liars."

"I think you should give Gavin another chance."

"What!" I sit up in bed. "How can you say that? He lied to me!"

"And then he explained it all in his letter," she says. "You like him a lot. I know you do. He made a mistake and he's trying to make up for it. You should meet him halfway."

My eyes flood with unshed tears. I think deep down I know she's right. I suffered when I found out about Gavin's lie. I was heartbroken. When I read his letter and realized that TJ also lied to me, I just wanted revenge. I wanted to tell him it was over and then be done with it. I didn't hurt at all.

"Gavin is the guy your heart wants," Livi continues. "You should talk to him."

I look at his letter and think about how he's been the last few weeks. He's quiet. He sits there and ignores the world, and then he leaves school for lunch. He doesn't seem to have any friends anymore. This entire thing has ruined his life lately. TJ still has his soccer team, his friends, and his reputation. He hasn't suffered at all, and yet the guy who was noble enough to admit he made a mistake has had all of the suffering heaped onto his shoulders.

When we get off the phone, I send Gavin a text.

Me: Hey, are you awake?

It's only eight-thirty so he has to be awake. But I sit around and wait for a reply that never comes.

Then I pull on the warmest clothes I own and go out to the living room. Mom is asleep but Grandpa is still up listening to the TV.

"Can I borrow your truck?" I ask him.

He frowns. "How late is it?"

"Not that late," I lie.

"Okay then. Be careful, it's cold out there."

"Thanks, Grandpa," I say, giving him a hug. "I'll be back soon."

CHAPTER TWENTY-FOUR

GAVIN

WITH ONE FINAL nail in place, I step back and admire my creation. The greenhouse is almost completely finished, and it only took about nine hours of straight work in the freezing cold.

I've never felt so freaking accomplished as I pull my gloves off my hands and tuck them into the sleeve of my jacket for warmth. I was only going to put the roof on tonight as a surprise for Clarissa, but after that was finished, I decided to attach the green wall panels. Then, the door. Then frame out the window in the door. Then I just kept going. The frigid cold was only quelled by moving around, so I kept moving.

Now the greenhouse stands tall and proud, brand new and untarnished. I'm standing outside, my tools sitting on top of the table I made.

The official plans for the greenhouse have shelves going all around the inside walls, but there's enough room for a table in the middle, something counter height so you can plant flowers or do work in there before you move it to its place against the wall. Clarissa had briefly mentioned how she'd like to have a table one day.

So I made one.

I exhale on my fingers in an attempt to warm them up, but it doesn't do much. I glance at my watch. It's just after midnight. First thing tomorrow morning when the stores are open, I'm going to find a gigantic bow, like what dealerships put on cars. I'll put it on the front door and then let Clarissa discover it on her own.

My heart warms at the idea, even though it's actually freezing.

Headlights blast against the greenhouse, the rumble of an engine following along behind it. I whip around, hoping it's not a cop coming to bust me for being out too late, but it's an older Chevy truck. I've seen it in Clarissa's driveway.

My heart races and I don't know why, but it feels like I've been caught doing something wrong. The truck shuts off and Clarissa tumbles out, walking quickly to me, her eyes wide.

"You finished it?" she shrieks. "Is it done? It looks done?" Her cheeks are pink, her expression bewildered. She looks so beautiful in the moonlight.

I laugh. "Yep. It's done."

"Why?" She throws her hands in the air, but she's not mad. She smiles as she looks over the greenhouse, running her fingers across the outside wall. "I told you to wait until it wasn't so cold."

I shrug. "The weather channel lied. It's totally not snowing."

She turns to me, her smile lighting me upside like it's Christmas morning. I realize why I did all this work tonight. For that smile. It was totally worth it.

"I made you a promise and I hated making you wait any longer to see it fulfilled."

She walks closer to me, her gaze never leaving mine until she notices the table I'm standing next to. "What's this?"

"It's a table, you know for the middle of the greenhouse? I heard you say you wanted one, so I looked up some building plans online and got some extra wood."

She places her palm on the tabletop. "It's perfect," she breathes, her words coming out in little clouds of white.

The next thing I know, she's throwing her arms around me. Her cheek is cold against mine, her thick jacket so puffy, she feels like a cloud as I wrap my arms nervously around her.

"Thank you," she says so softly I barely hear it. "Thank you for this."

"Don't thank me," I say, still holding onto her, my eyes closed as I soak up her presence like it's all the fuel I'll never need to survive. "I should thank you for not killing me when you found out what I did."

She pulls away slowly, then gazes up at me. "I read your letter."

I don't know what to say, so I glance down and then at the greenhouse, suddenly unable to meet her gaze.

"Thank you for writing it," she says, taking a step back. "I ended things with TJ."

"That was...probably for the best," I say.

She snorts. "Yeah. Honestly, I didn't even like him. I just—"

"You just what?" I say. It suddenly means a lot to me to know exactly how she felt about my former friend.

She shrugs. "I wanted to like him because he liked me.

He didn't have a problem with my height, and he was nice and—"

"Your height?" I ask.

She shrugs, one hand holding onto her elbow. "My last boyfriend broke up with me because I was too tall."

"That's bullshit," I say, as anger warms my insides. What a dick. Who would throw away a girl as amazing as Clarissa just because she was a little taller than average? I walk closer to her, standing tall, until I'm just a few inches away and have to look down on her. I pat the top of her head. "You look pretty short to me."

She grins and looks down. "I think I was just so happy to have connected with you, that when you hurt me, I tried to connect with someone else as soon as possible." She exhales. "It did not work. It was stupid."

"I'm really sorry for everything," I say softly, wishing I could be wrapped in one of her hugs again. Instead, I settle for reaching out and letting my fingers graze her arm. "I had a connection with you, too. Before I ruined it all, you were very special to me."

Clarissa's jaw shivers as she looks up at me. "You're too cold," I say. "You should get back home and warm up. I don't want you getting sick."

She shakes her head. "I'm fine. Plus," She holds up her finger. "Wait here, I brought something."

She rushes back to her truck and then comes back with two cups from the Lone Star Diner. "It's not as good as Mrs. Bradley's homemade hot chocolate, but it's still pretty good."

Steam rises from the lid as she hands one to me.

"You just happened to have two hot chocolates in your truck?"

"It's my grandpa's truck," she says, followed by, "And well, I thought you might be here after you didn't answer my text."

"You texted me?" My heart races at the thought. I've spent all night out here alone thinking she wasn't thinking about me at all. "My phone has been in my truck so I wouldn't break it around all these tools. What'd you say?"

"Nothing," she says. "Just wanted to talk. When you didn't answer, I came to find you."

"What do you want to talk about?" I ask. I cradle the Styrofoam cup in my hands, letting the steam rise up and warm my face.

"Well..." She's shivering so much she can barely talk.

"Hold that thought," I say. I pull open my passenger door. "Get in."

Then I climb into my side and crank the engine, turning up the heater. This truck has one hell of a heater, and within seconds, the cab starts warming up.

"Mmm," she says, leaning her face toward the air vent. "This is much better. Grandpa's heater sucks. I was halfway here before it started getting even a little warm."

I try not to be so stupid-eyed as I watch her, but it's hard because I'm totally crazy about this girl. "Not to be pushy, but you were about to say something."

She smiles, her eyes closed while the hot air warms her face. "I'm sorry about the trouble you have at home, with your dad and everything. I had no idea."

"No one does," I say. "I keep that shit locked up tight."

She looks over at me with sorrow in her eyes. "I've been thinking about what happened, and I don't really blame you. If I were you, I think I would have lied too. I mean...we had this amazing date and—" She takes a breath and I am on the edge of my seat dying to hear what she'll say next. "I mean, it's not like you could have told me right there on the beach. I know I wouldn't have. And...it's not like you destroyed my greenhouse knowing it was mine."

She turns a sharp look toward me. "I don't condone senseless violence, though."

I bark out a laugh. "Trust me, I don't either. I can't believe I did that. I've *never* done anything like that."

She sips from her hot chocolate, and I watch her. Now that she's here in my truck with me, all I can do is watch her, grateful for every second of time she gives me.

"My grandmother used to work at the daycare," she says after a while. "That greenhouse was her passion project. We have lots of photos of her with the greenhouse, showing flowers and plants to the kids. She actually died a long time ago, so I never knew her, but when I started working at the daycare, Grandpa told me about it."

A knot tightens in my stomach. Shit.

She glances at me briefly before looking back at the cup in her hands. "I asked Mrs. Bradley if I could fix the old greenhouse and make it new again so I could give the kids a greenhouse just like my grandma did. I spent all summer building it with my grandpa."

"Shit, Clarissa," I breathe. "I'm so sorry. I feel like such an ass."

A small grin plays on her lips. "Then you won't want to hear this next part."

I stiffen. Her eyes are pained, her knuckles white as she grips her cup. "Grandpa has glaucoma and he's been slowly going blind. That greenhouse is the last project he ever made, and it was our project that we did together. So...I know it belongs to the daycare, but it's really my greenhouse. It means the world to me."

I rub my fingers across my forehead. "God, I'm so sorry."

Her fingers are warm when she touches my arm. "It's okay, Gavin. You didn't know."

"I—" I look at her beautiful face, that soft knowing smile on her lips, the dip of her brows as she watches me. "I can never make this up to you," I say.

She shakes her head. "You already did. It's done. It's finished. I didn't tell you this to make you feel bad, I just wanted you to know the whole story."

Her hand slides down to mine, her fingers effortlessly tucking between mine, as we hold onto each other in the space between us. "You told me your whole story in your letter, and I wanted you to know mine."

I squeeze her hand. "My dad got his job back. His boss also talked him into attending AA meetings so...we're cautiously optimistic."

"That's amazing," she says, squeezing my hand. "My uncle goes to AA and it literally saved his life. He's been sober for years now."

"That's good. Maybe this will help my dad. But now that he's working, I don't have to work as much at my job."

"That's why you insisted on finishing the greenhouse this weekend?" she asks.

I nod. She slides over, setting her cup in the cup holder underneath my radio. I do the same to mine, and the next thing I know, Clarissa is sitting right next to me, her leg touching mine, her hand still holding mine as she brings it to her lap.

"Do you think we could put this behind us?" she asks softly. Her head rests against my shoulder as we stare at the greenhouse in front of us.

"I would love that," I say.

I let my cheek lean against the top of her head and we sit like this for a long while, the only sound is the heater and the soft rumble of the engine.

I close my eyes and enjoy the moment, feel the swell of happiness that's growing inside of me. I don't deserve this girl at all, but it looks like she's giving me another chance. Life could not be any better than this.

"Hey, look," Clarissa whispers.

I open my eyes. Tiny white drops of snow hit the windshield and then melt away. "It's snowing," she says, sitting up.

I turn to her. "Good thing the greenhouse is finished."

She grins. "This feels special."

"It feels like a moment," I say, wondering if she remembers what we'd said that day at the beach.

"A good moment," she says back, her eyes narrowing mischievously at me.

This time I don't think too long or wait for a signal, because I don't want the perfect moment to slip away. I cradle her cheek in my hand and lower my lips to hers. And then the greatest thing ever happens.

She kisses me back.

CHAPTER TWENTY-FIVE

Clarissa

"IT'S COLD!" Regan says. She crosses her little arms over her chest and pouts up at me. "Ms. Clarissa, it's too cold out here!"

I lean forward, putting my hands on my knees so I'm eye level with the three year old. "Remember what we talked about inside?"

She shakes her head. That's probably because she was too busy playing with the sparkles on her shoes. "We talked about how a greenhouse is what?"

She thinks about it for a moment. "Green?"

"Well, yes, but that's not all." I stand up and look over my group of seven kids. "Who thinks it's cold out here?"

They all raise their hands. "Who remembers what it's like inside the greenhouse?"

"Hot!" a five-year-old named Gabriella says.

I nod. "Yep! It's cold out here, but our greenhouse is nice and warm inside. That way we can grow our flowers no matter what the weather is like outside." I hold up the tulip bulb my grandpa had given me weeks ago. "Are we ready to plant our first one?"

A chorus excitement fills the air. "Who remembers what this is called?"

"A bulb!" Gabriella says.

"Yep, it's a bulb. Great job. Let's go plant it!"

The kids walk in a single file line across the grass and to my new greenhouse, which looks amazing in the daylight. Inside, I have them stand around the table, all facing the clay pot in the center.

We talk about the proper way to plant a tulip bulb and I let each kid take turns covering it with potting soil. I'm not exactly a plant expert, but I did to a ton of research on tulips last night, so I tell them everything I learned.

"Someone's here," Jabir says. He points to the door.

I walk over and look out the small window in the door. Gavin backs his truck up to the greenhouse. When he gets out, he waves at me and then walks to the tailgate drapes an arm over it.

"Hold on a minute," I tell the kids. "Jabir, will you be the leader?"

He nods eagerly and holds open the door to the greenhouse while I step outside.

"What's all this?" I ask Gavin.

"Can you bring the kids out here?" he says.

I call for them and they all rush up beside me, forming a semi-circle around Gavin's tailgate. "This is my friend Gavin," I say. The kids say hello to him and he grins back.

"Have you planted the tulip yet?" he asks.

Last night, while talking on the phone and staying up way too late, I'd told Gavin about the tulip bulb my grandpa gave me, and how today we were going to plant it in the greenhouse. I can't believe he remembered.

"We just did," I say.

"It's a flower," one of the kids says.

Gavin puts his hands on his hips as he addresses the kids. "Did you all pay attention to Ms. Clarissa's instructions?"

"Yes!" they shout back.

"Do you think you could do it again?"

"Yes!"

I lift an eyebrow. "What are you talking about?"

Gavin lowers his tailgate, revealing small bags of potting soil, clay pots, and a bag of tulip bulbs. "I brought enough for your whole class to plant their own tulip," he says sheepishly. "Is that okay?"

I have to bite on the inside of my lip to keep from smiling like a crazy person.

The kids cheer and jump around and rush to the back of his truck to get a better look. I give him a quick hug. "You are the best."

He grins down at me, then places a quick kiss on my forehead.

"Eww!" someone says, which only makes me blush harder.

"This greenhouse is going to be your legacy," he says, giving a bag of soil to each kid. "I just wanted to do something to help."

It's been a week since Gavin finished my greenhouse in the middle of the night. We've been pretty much inseparable ever since. I've been happier than I could ever imagine, and yet sometimes there's this little nagging feeling in my chest when I'm lying awake at night. This feeling that tells me maybe something bad will happen. Maybe he'll change his mind.

But then Gavin goes and does something like this, and I realize he's the best boyfriend a girl could ever have.

"Hey," I say, poking him in the stomach while the kids take turns picking a tulip bulb from the bag. "I think you're amazing."

"Oh yeah?" Gavin licks his lips, then lowers his mouth to my ear. "Because I think I'm in love."

ABOUT THE AUTHOR

Amy Sparling is the bestselling author of books for teens and the teens at heart. She lives on the coast of Texas with her family, her spoiled rotten pets, and a huge pile of books. She graduated with a degree in English and has worked at a bookstore, coffee shop, and a fashion boutique. Her fashion skills aren't the best, but luckily she turned her love of coffee and books into a writing career that means she can work in her pajamas. Her favorite things are coffee, book boyfriends, and Netflix binges.

She's always loved reading books from R. L. Stine's Fear Street series, to The Baby Sitter's Club series by Ann, Martin, and of course, Twilight. She started writing her own books in 2010 and now publishes several books a year. Amy loves getting messages from her readers and responds to every single one! Connect with her on one of the links below.

Website: AmySparling.com

Instagram: @writeamysparling

Goodreads: goodreads.com/Amy_Sparling

Wattpad: AmySparlingWrites

www.ingramcontent.com/pod-product-compliance
Ingram Content Group UK Ltd.
Pitfield, Milton Keynes, MK11 3LW, UK
UKHW040022200726
13854UKWH00001B/306

9 798201 844417